JULIE
LAVENDER

MRS.
AMAZING
AND
THE SEED

ISBN: 978-1-54395-058-8

Dedicated to Mrs. A's Cheering Section

Mark, Jean-Marc, Christian, Amiee, Tina, Matt, Sierra, Josiah,
Levi, Kendra, Ryan, Jillene, Pam, Emily, Belle, Kayla, Tamara,
Levi, Megan, Caroline, Alexander, Gena, Amy, Kelly, Elena, Chaya and Lynda.

PROLOGUE

THEY WERE TRANSMIGRATING, FILTERING IN AND OUT OF spaces and pathways as if moving through the hidden doors in a funhouse maze. Passing through layers of time and dimension, the voyagers felt themselves sinking down, deeper and deeper, into an atmosphere that grew denser and darker with each passing moment. There were flashes of light, and cloudy mists through which they traveled toward an inevitable destination — a destination they desperately wished they would never have to reach.

"Heeere *they* commme! Thossse sssssickening *Wwwon-der-erssss!*" A brittle, hissing voice spit the words out with such disgust as though it was choking on the gall of its own hatred.

"It isss farrr worsssseee than we antisss-ipated!" A spying scout screeched in revulsion, alarming many others who had hidden themselves in the shadows.

"The He and She and the sssspppawn of *their* Generationssss have . . . Sseedssss!"

Now the entire cohort was in full battle alert. Their commander shrieked:

"They mussst be neutralizzzed before it'ss too late. The Pressscribed Order mussst not be quessstioned!"

Razor-sharp shafts and thorns were unsheathed and aimed with chilling accuracy. Deadly in their subtlety, these weapons were cunningly designed to leave wounds that would go undetected. Each one inflicted just enough discomfort to penetrate its victim and unleash an insidious flow of refined destruction, but never produced enough pain to actually reveal the true nature of its immense threat.

Sensing the growing danger, the unsuspecting travelers felt as though they would suffocate in the dread that was quickly engulfing them. Sizzling sounds pierced the air as the darts hit their marks and the thorns and brambles about them scratched their vulnerable flesh. Each prick implanted poisonous invading thoughts that would soon grow to choke out all sprouting opposition.

"You've been tricked!"

"Give up your silly fantasssiess."

"You are forsssssssaken."

"It'ssssss all your fault . . ."

Creepy voices whispered cruel thoughts, gleefully inflicting their venomous little torments.

"You are on your own."

"You cannot trussst in these mythsss!"

"You have failed . . ."

"No Purposssssseeee to thissss . . ."

The voyagers let loose cries of panic and dismay with the penetration of each pernicious word.

Cheering with glee, the attackers retreated into the periphery, gloating over the impact of their warcraft. Victory was surely at hand. If these meddlesome interlopers did not resist, they would soon drift into acquiescence. Watching with evil anticipation, the assailants were thrilled to see their victims succumbing to a lethal mixture of doubt, fear, and depression.

"Successsssss!" came the jubilant hisses. They were certain they would prevail.

Suddenly, a string of their curses filled the atmosphere. The He and his boy-spawn were putting up a fight! With them victory could not be assured. At least not, yet.

But the She and the girl-spawn were another matter. They had failed to resist.

CHAPTER 1
Snot, Slobber, and Salty Sobs

FAYE FAULTSOM GULPED DOWN THE LUMP IN HER THROAT and held her breath. She hoped, desperately, that this would shut off the leaking hose behind her eyeballs which threatened to flood her tear ducts and leave her in a snotty puddle. She sat across from Constance, her oldest daughter, whose restrained anger and carefully chosen words cut her as much as any tongue-lashing might have. Nothing prepared Faye for the words Constance squeezed out of her knotted insides that evening.

"It wasn't a childhood I remember particularly fondly, Mom. And . . . I don't believe

. . . in *your* imaginary world . . . anymore . . . "

As she exhaled, the fifty-year-old mother of four felt as though tectonic plates were shifting within her. She would not be able to swallow the resulting tsunami of tears, nor keep it from bursting over her shores, once she heard Constance's car pull out of the family driveway as the sun set that evening. Those few words, along with other revelations that her daughter painstakingly parceled out, left Faye no place to hide. She could not escape the reality that her hopes of nourishing and protecting the garden of her daughter's heart were somehow ruined.

Inside, she felt a hollow reverberation of pain followed by the knowledge that something along the way had crushed her daughter's imagination, the *one thing* Faye had tried to nurture and guard the most fiercely in her children. Where had they, where had *she*, gone wrong? A flood of emotion roiled inside her, churning up images and memories of her own barren childhood, uprooting her dreams for Constance and disorienting her. She lay in the dark for hours going over and over things in her mind, as her husband slept soundly next to her.

"Oh, Honey, it's just a separation thing," he had said. "She just needs to find herself and be her own person . . . don't overreact . . . "

Her husband's solid logic was, of course, the most clearheaded way to see things, for every family has its blemishes and rough patches. Of course they had made their mistakes as parents — many of them! As for Faye, there were lots of things Constance could find to criticize about her mothering. But Faye knew something deeper and more alarming was at work.

Mrs. Faultsom could not shake the strange feeling that some dark thing had taken root in Constance and, having dug itself deep into her being, had sprung up and wrapped itself tightly around her heart. Now the light in Constance's eyes had dimmed. She was growing detached and distant. Angry. Cold. She had ceased to believe in *Wonder*.

It was an uproarious tangle of red curls and wet freckles that met her pillow that night as Faye lay her head down. She drew her legs up to her chest and huddled under the comforter. Frank snored determinedly as she dabbed her eyes, stifled her sobs, and blew her marathon-running nose on the ball of tissues she pulled out of her nightgown sleeve. Easily moved to tears, Faye could always find a place to pocket away a stash of hankies.

Her only comfort was the snuffling of the family hound dog, Cornelius, as he rooted his way back up and out of the covers from the bottom of the bed for a fresh breath of midnight air. As if sensing her distress, the dog panted excitedly and gave Faye a sloppy, sliding kiss on her cheek before returning to his spot down under the covers. At least she couldn't fail Cornie.

Wiping off his slobber and the salt from her dribbling tears, Faye flipped back through the pages of their lives, to the time when she had met her husband and they had both discovered the existence of the strange and mystical realm of *Wonder* together. She had always loved to hear the deep and reassuring sound of Frank's voice recounting the details of their courtship to their children. Tonight, that was a safe place for Mrs. Faultsom to begin reviewing her life, with recollections of a season full of the promise of their courtship and their intriguing revelations.

CHAPTER 2
A Curious Courtship

LITTLE SIX-YEAR-OLD CONSTANCE FAULTSOM CURLED UP IN her daddy's lap and asked to hear the story once more. "Dada, tell me again how you and mama met and why ya liked 'er? Didn'tcha think she was kinda silly at first?"

Frank, a bit taken aback, chuckled.

"Well, yes, your Mama has always been pretty unique but *that's* what makes her so special."

"Tell me again 'bout the funny things she always wored."

"Ok, yes, your mom wore these puffy deals that she tucked into her . . . ah . . . blouses. They were kind of like what football players wear under their uniforms to make their shoulders so big and bulky."

"Boulder Pads?" Connie tried to name them.

"No, sweetie. *Shoulder* pads. Everybody wore them back then. People thought they were pretty stylish, but now that I think about it, I guess they *did* make your mama look a bit funny."

Constance giggled and begged Frank to continue. "Daddy, tell me the whole story 'n' tell it the *wight* way . . . "

Franklin Farnsworth Faultsom, with his thick dark hair, mustache, and tortoise-shell glasses, crowned by a set of thoughtfully expressive eyebrows, had a flare for formality. A student of ancient civilizations, he always told the tale of his and Faye's courtship as though he were narrating an impressive piece of world history. Even though most of it was beyond her comprehension, little Constance loved to hear the sound of his big descriptive words. Even when she didn't know what they all meant, she somehow understood them because her daddy had a way of telling this particular story that his little girl adored.

"Ah huummm . . . " Clearing his throat to set the stage, he would thus begin.

"Young twenty-something, buttoned-down Franklin Farnsworthy Faultsom, who sported wingtip shoes and bulky cable-knit sweaters, with spiffy bold patterns on them, was amused and intrigued by the offbeat and breezy personality of Miss Faye Andoria Green. He first encountered her at a local plant nursery one fine April morning as she selected flower varieties. He found her quirky way of talking to the seeds as she chose them to be more than a little charming.

"Although he could have had his pick of the maidens from his upper-crust circles, he found this mod-bohemian nymph quite captivating, and he pursued the redhead with her shoulder pads, wild curls, bangles, and irrepressible idealism.

"It wasn't long before Frank and Faye realized that they both *saw* things, odd little things — often out of the corners of their eyes. They would sometimes sense that something *other* was whispering to them through a portal that hung open in the air. At times it was as if a breeze had blown in from another room . . . no, from another *realm*.

"And they both *knew* things; things one doesn't know with just the mind alone, but things that lit them up on the inside, as if someone had let fireflies loose in their stomachs. They knew there was another dimension. More than that, they both sensed that something or someone from *there* was beckoning them to enter.

"But alas, few in their world believed in true *Mystery* anymore, and it was very much analyzed and "pooh-poohed," as if belief in the miraculous was some sort of intellectual or psychological deficiency.

It was fashionable only to think in terms of the concrete and the 'prove-able.' Rational minds simply denied the existence of nonmaterial realities, attributing them to chemical reactions in the brains of those who reported them."

"Some people, however, did feel the absence of true mystery in their daily existences and sought to conjure up fantastical worlds to enter, as they peered into the dark depths of their own cogitations and those of would-be mediums and mystics. These diversions pacified many. But when Faye and Frank compared these phenomena to their own encounters, they found them to be the stuff of sideshows, magic tricks — or worse. Some people embraced the substance of a chilling, gray reality that sought to snuff out the firefly glow of any true marvels. Sometimes it seemed as though Frank and Faye were the last people on earth who actually saw the authentic miracles hidden in the invisible.

"When they first met, the couple spoke tentatively of these things although, as she felt Frank's reassuring gaze and quiet confirmations pave the way, Faye would often jump into the deep end of things before she could stop herself. It wasn't long before they were comparing notes about their experiences and it was with great relief and delight that Faye would exclaim:

"Oh! I thought it was just me! *You've* felt that? *You've* seen it, too?"

So began their rather odd courtship. And then one day, they both found their way to some *distant* place together, and when they did, they knew they had also found each other."

"Did he kiss her then, Daddy? Were you, was *he* tewwibly womantic? Constance would interrupt.

"Why, of course, he was and *is* . . . *tewwibly womantic*. And yes, I . . . er . . . *he* kissed her and told her he couldn't live without her, for they shared special secrets — intriguing things that they both knew no one else seemed to understand."

"So he mawwied her!" Constance would squeal with delight, Frank nodding as she prodded him to continue.

"Daddy, tell me about the special seecwets now! What stuff happened to them?"

"Well, lots of strange things happened to them. Things that seemed like invitations to a party in another world. And they called that world *Wonder*, because there just wasn't another word for it."

At this point Frank would do his best to explain to his daughter what he himself found quite perplexing and utterly inexplicable. To his relief, little Constance was often nodding off at this point in the story, just as her daddy started to dither around in his attempt to describe what he and Faye had experienced.

Once Constance was dozing soundly, Frank would often sit with his daughter cradled in his arms, thinking about what was at stake. Even though there was much that he himself didn't totally comprehend, he knew *Wonder* was worth fighting for. Considering this, his heart would swell with tenderness as he thought back to the moment with Faye that had forever set his course.

As young sweethearts Faye and Frank had been walking hand-in-hand late one fall day as the soft glow of the evening sky ignited briefly with the sun's last wink before it slid below the horizon. A chilly breeze caused them both to shudder. Faye was chattering with excitement about her latest precarious pursuit of exploration. A consuming desire for *Wonder* filled her soul. She was running headlong into the unknown without hesitation.

"It was like I was in two places at once, all day! It was so weird and yet *so* normal. I couldn't figure out which place seemed more real, and I can't shake the feeling that this whole thing is so much bigger than we are. And . . . Franky, you are the only person I've ever met who understands. No one else seems to get it at all. I just can't make myself fit in and *I don't want to*."

Now a breeze of uncertainty chilled Frank's heart.

She was such a handful, this Faye Green. So passionate and willing to go out on a limb. He knew that a life with her would be far from ordinary and would surely upset the apple cart of any predictability. He let go of her hand. Although he, too, felt a calling from somewhere beyond himself, sometimes Faye scared him. Frank had always had a clear and conventional life mapped out before him. Success was just around the corner if he stayed on track. But Faye was anything but conventional, and she had this way of always drawing him into unchartered waters. A life with her would never allow him to fit the mold he had always been expected to fill. Where were they really heading?

Thinking that he'd better distance himself from the fetching redhead with whom he was so smitten, Frank turned to look at her. He was just about to put the brakes on things with Faye, when he was suddenly overcome with a feeling of destiny, as times, spaces, and faces flashed before his mind's eye. A welcoming pandemonium unfolded in which there were voices of children shouting, singing a very odd song, and giggling wildly. He felt himself whooshed upward, and then sliding straight down. He was experiencing a panorama of weird sounds and smells, of reverberating music, dancing lights, and a bizarre, fuzzy yellowness. Feelings he couldn't name overtook him. It all happened so swiftly that he wasn't able to process these impressions, but he *felt* Faye there in each and every layer of sensation as he stood looking into her verdant green eyes. Then it all quickly vanished.

A few moments later he heard himself speak.

"We are *intended* to be together. There is so much more to discover, and we *have* to find it *together*."

This came as a revelation to him from his own lips.

"Franklin Farnsworth Faultsom, are you proposing?" Faye blurted out as her verdant greens welled up with tears.

"Why, yes, I guess I am . . . Faye Andoria Green."

Flinging herself at the tall, solid man who stood before her, Faye threw her arms around him and melted into his chest. As Frank enfolded her in his arms, Faye felt they were both transported to a vast field of fragrant colors stretching beyond the horizon in every direction. It was so glorious that it filled her with awe. Now she was bawling and desperately searching for tissues as her nose unleashed its slimy goo.

"Oh! There goes my nose! What a mess I must be!" How Faye wished she could be one of those graceful, elegant creatures she so admired. But this was not to be. As she looked up at him, Frank daubed her cheeks dry with his sleeve cuff and kissed her nose. He gazed at that adorable speckled face of hers and caught glimpses of his children to come, emerging like butterflies from the cocoon of a very unusual way of life that he knew simply had to be.

It had to be, but it would not be easy. In their now inevitable quest for *Wonder*, Faye and Frank would be navigating through hostile seas.

CHAPTER 3
An Irregular Family

"AAAHH! WE ARE SSSSOOO CLOSSSSE, MY SSSSPLENDID DIS-sss-im-u-latorssss."

From the shadows, a group of conspirators watched the goings-on below them with obsessive interest.

"If we can keep the grown humansssss busssy and disssstracted, they will yield their offsssssspring to our influencessss!" The leader hissed with anticipation, licking its lips as if ready to tear into a savory piece of meat.

"We will ssssoon have a world in which few quesssstion and even *fewer* ex-ssssplore beyond the borderssss we sssset for them." Another watcher added, shuddering at the dangers they faced if their plans to contain the humans failed.

"The fleshcarriersssss are ssssooo in-ssssipidly ssssstupid — eas-sssily presssssured to conform to The Pressssscribed Order — under the right circumsssstancessss," the anxious watcher added, reassuring itself that everything was under control.

The commander nodded in agreement.

"Yessss. They will, indeed, accept ssssamnessss of thinking . . . *if* we can get at them early. It issss ab-ssssolutely necessssary to possesss their ssssspawn . . . it isss *all* about the little onessss."

☞☞☞☞☞☞☞

Bravely embarking into the unknown, the quirky courtship of young Frank and Faye quickly grew into an enduring partnership in which the soon married Mr. and Mrs. Faultsom wasted no time in pursuing *Wonder* together. Then, in just the blink of an eye, their children came along and, naturally, the Faultsoms talked often to them of their *Wonderly* pursuits and belief in the mysteries that everyone they knew seemed to discount and scoff at. Despite disapproving outside forces, Faye and Frank taught their children to adventure and "imagine-ate," asking: How? Why not? What if?

"Let's just *suppose*," they would exclaim, "and let's discover the possibilities!"

And, oh my, each of the Faultsom children were quite the firecrackers! And their mom and dad were determined to light their little fuses so they could burst into *Wonder*'s sparkling world of incredibilities, despite the fact that this was viewed as quite abnormal by the parents and townspeople around them. It was precisely because of this, that Faye and Frank were soon facing a mounting threat. You see, although it was expected of them, they decided that they absolutely would not surrender their children to the facilitators of the local Center for Child Development and Life Preparation. These were the people who were in charge of making sure all children were developing in "alignment with The Prescribed Order." Faye and Frank were quite alarmed by the way children were being pressured to accept a way of thinking and believing that seemed to be smothering any possibility of *Wondering*. The local Center was another one of what the Faye and Frank referred to as "Grown-Up Factories," that were poised on the prominent corners in practically every community. Mr. and Mrs. Faultsom knew that these places were somehow killing the imaginations of the children who were left there for any length of time. At all costs, *their* kids must *not* be subjected to The Grown-Up Factory, for The GUPF's, as they called them, had nearly killed their own capacity for *Wonderment* years before.

When she was a little girl and The Prescribed Order was beginning to gain wide acceptance, Faye had flitted up to her GUPF facilitator one day, bubbling over with stories of the faraway frontiers she visited in her imagination. When the facilitator couldn't convince her that these experiences were nonsense and not to be believed in, Faye was sent away with a big black X-mark pinned to her blouse and a note advising her parents to take her in hand or there would be consequences. Little Faye had cried all the way home only to be scolded by her mother and father who warned her not to talk about such things ever again. Despite this, she did not stop believing. Frank was also given the mental version of a knuckle-knocking slap across the back of his hand for expressing a belief that did not align his facilitator's "appropriate opinion." Imaginative thinking was *not* an approved part of The Prescribed Order or it's central plan.

Now, on any given morning, the Faultsoms would see neighborhood kids climbing into transport vehicles, being carried away and led into sterile-looking buildings for hours and hours at a time. The couple took note of these children with grave concern as they came home terribly perturbed, cross, and out of sorts. Faye could sometimes overhear them talk about how the kids at The GUPF would practically eat each other up at the lunch tables.

Frank and Faye also knew that there were tests, assessments, and evaluations given to the children in the factories and, as a result, the kids were beaten down and sort of shriveled up inside. It seemed that the experts at The GUPF were always trying to get the children to prove something or other about what was being impressed upon them, while never giving them the space and time to "suppose" about anything truly interesting at all. The factory facilitators were also fond of saying things like:

"Your poor parents and grandparents simply aren't equipped to understand what *we* know *you* understand. After all, since *they* were kids, we humans have made so much progress. We clearly don't need the old traditions, ancient myths, and silly fancies *they* believed in anymore."

This alarmed the Faultsoms who had discovered echoes of their own supernatural experiences buried in the memories of the aged. They had encountered more than a few old folks who seemed to know all about *Wonder*. However, these people were often called "feeble-minded" by the factory facilitators who said that they should be ignored. But my! Such radiance flickered in eyes of these elderly explorers. Faye and Frank loved to hear their remembrances and catch glimpses of *Wonder* itself on their faces.

One afternoon, the couple came upon a very enchanting little old lady ambling down a country road. She wore a big, floppy, daisy-covered hat and a set of purple galoshes, although the day was clear and sunny. Tickled by the skip in her step and the way she would frequently stop in her tracks, gaze at the sky, and let loose an adorable giggle, Faye and Frank slowed the pace of their bike ride and stopped to introduce themselves to the elderly sprite. As they approached, they could hear her singing a haunting bit of a tune that was, after every few phrases, punctuated by her tinkling laughter.

"Miss Filippa" was quite happy to make their acquaintance, but after no more than a moment of small talk, she curtseyed blithely and took her leave. Apparently uninterested in social conventions, she seemed happily absorbed in her own world . . . or in some other. Just a few paces down the road, however, she stopped abruptly, turned about, and addressed Faye and Frank most earnestly.

"You know, my dears, when I was a child, we had wide-open spaces to explore . . . in our thoughts and beyond! Why, we could go awanderin' and aponderin' to the edge of the universe and back, just to see what there was to see. We found things that your generation has lost. No . . . That isn't so! These things haven't been *lost*, they've been *hidden*. They've been teaching children *not to see* for decades now . . . and teaching you all not to listen to those of us who *do* see. But . . . *I* shall go on seeing . . . no matter what *they* say! "

At this, she took up her little tune once again and skipped away down the road, leaving the Faultsoms standing there stirred to tears. They knew Miss Filippa was right, for the kids who went to factories had, for the most part, lost their trust in the stories their grandparents had to tell and even the guidance their parents had to give. They seemed to be in training to become human cogs in some sort of universal machine, without the time to stop and ask what they were doing, or why. Worst of all, the kids who came out of The Grown-Up Factories seemed to have had their inner "believers" disconnected.

No, this simply would not do for the Faultsom children. For even though Frank and Faye had never been all the way *in*, they had experienced enough to know that *Wonder* did exist and they just *knew* that it was filled with mind-boggling, brain-exploding treasures waiting to be explored and contemplated. They were insistent that their very unique and curious children, Constance, Charleston, Chance, and Chief would not be pressured to conform.

This decision, however, not only made the Faultsom family social stand-outs, but also alienated Frank's parents, Fredrick and Regina Faultsom, who were thoroughly conventional. They grew cold and distant toward their son because of his embarrassing belief in *Wonder* and his marriage to Faye, whom they considered to be quite unsuitable and far beneath their son's status. And, when the children came along, Fredrick and Regina became increasingly agitated about Frank's and Faye's unorthodox parenting decisions.

"Oh, that odd, odd girl!" Regina would cry as her gravely disappointed husband would shake his head.

"Yes, my dear, it would seem that she has ruined our Franklin. He has simply lost his senses. How can he allow her to poison the children with all of that *Wonder* nonsense!" Frederick would gripe.

But despite his parents' vocal disapproval, Frank could not be deterred from forging a way forward for his family that would preserve and protect the extraordinary beauty he found in their unusual way of life, but this proved to be a very costly choice.

For having stepped out of line, Frank lost his father's endorsement and came under the suspicions of many of those in the elite circles in which he had spent his youth. He was even discretely dismissed from his position in a well-respected enterprise because his boss concluded that Frank simply wasn't "one of them" any longer. Following this, he ran into many an abruptly closed door, until at long last, he did find work as a product designer at the lowly Peerless Pencil Company (The PP) and made a go of it there. For a man of Frank's education and ability this was a bitter pill to swallow, but he was resolute about his convictions and would not turn back, no matter how much his parents and peers pressured him. No matter what it cost him, he would not force his family to "fit in." So, off to The PP he went to make his way in the world.

Knowing that his burgeoning little family was often misunderstood and looked down upon, Frank built a fence around the wild and woodsy garden of their funky vintage Dumble Street house to keep out the prying neighborhood snoops, as Faye took over the supervision of the kids' education. With inexhaustible enthusiasm, Frank's untamed bride threw herself into the possibility of all that *Wonder* might offer their children. Transforming the Faultsom home into an expeditionary launching pad, each morning she pointed the kids toward new heights of discovery and hit the ignition button. And when, one by one, they returned from their flights of fancy she would gather them up in her arms and squeal with delight at each childish adventure story recounted.

"Oh myyyy! What a magical morning you have had, dear heart's! Was it terribly tickly when that ladybug inspected your fingers?" Faye giggled as if she was being tickled herself.

"Did you really hear her singing as she opened up her spotted shell and stretched out her wings? Why, of course you did! Did she say goodbye before she flew off? No? Well, ladybugs *can* be very rude . . . they tend to be quite proud of those spots and you know what it's like when one is too impressed with oneself."

Faye was often moved to tears as she drank in the oceans of green and blue there in the wide eyes of her untainted and trusting little ones. No child of hers would wear a black X upon their hearts if she had anything to say about it. She and Frank would do their level best to protect Constance, Charleston, Chance, and Chief from the kinds of wounds they had received from the imagination-crushers in their own lives. No matter what, they would carve out a space in which their kids could embrace the extraordinary. And so it was that Mr. and Mrs. Faultsom grew a very irregular family, making sure that in addition to reading, writing, history, and math, the kids had hours of free time to noodle, explore, experiment, and go with Mom on her very unconventional "field trips" into unknown realms.

The kids also relished their time with Dad, especially when they got to go with him on his jaunts to the local warehouse store. These outings inevitably turned into something more like "retail safaris" on which they would bag the big game of industrial lots of toilet paper and canned chili. It was on these expeditions that Dad had a way of keeping the children grounded and of letting them know that he supported Faye's fanciful approach to family life. For you see, ever the more gregarious one of the two, Faye delighted in coming up with new itineraries for her husband and family to try out — attempting trips in and out of *Wonder* from various places.

Frank would often chuckle and shake his head as his wife pitched another one of her goofy schemes to push the envelope of their confidence and experience in these unexplored lands. He reeled her in, from time to time, lending his sound wisdom and quiet confidence as he learned, through the years, to support and gently temper her daring spirit. And when he didn't, it could be more than a bit chaotic at the Faultsoms'.

One famous episode went down in the annals of the family's history as quite a funny failure. While the kids in The GUPF's were often stuck droning The Prescribed Order songs they were fed everyday, Faye enrolled her kids in yodeling classes to help them channel their rambunctiousness, hoping that this somewhat kooky vocal enrichment exercise would turn their kids' constant vociferousness into something of a skill. She envisioned her young mountaineers hiking and singing as they summited snowcapped peaks, and jumped off into *Wonder's* waiting arms with their voices echoing through the canyons of their fancies.

Within days of his children's first yodeling lesson, their long-suf-
fering father put an end to further yodeling when he simply could
not take another "Diddly-odely-oh" from his enthusiastic warblers.
But he could not contain the silly jokes that the kids repeated over
and over for days!

"Knock knock!"

"Who's there?"

"Little Old Lady!"

"Littleoldladywho — hooo-hooo???

"Didley-oh Doh — doo-hee — heee-heeee!" The kids would
crack up as they bounced around the room.

Such was the unsuppressed silliness of a typical Faultsom free-
for-all, so Frank figured he needed to keep a firmer hand on the tiller
of their family's direction. But in this instance, it was far too late.
The kids' heads were all crammed full of "Littleoldladywhoooos!"
for weeks afterward and these produced welcome distractions for
them from regular schoolwork which, of course, tended to distress
their parents. From that time forward, Frank and Faye could often
be found talking long into the evening, after the children had gone

to bed, mulling over the latest *Wonder*-filled predicaments they had skirted. Together they plotted their next adventures and brainstormed about ways to navigate the often threatening waters of the world outside their home's harbor.

Cautiously optimistic about the possibilities that lay before them, Frank headed out each day to "slay the dragons" at The PP. Planting a kiss upon each of his dear Faultsoms, he drove off to take on his pressured-filled penciling, while Faye and the kids got on with the business of *Wondering*.

CHAPTER 4

Struggles, Strategies, and "The Song"

SHELL-SHOCKED BY THE FALLOUT OF HER OLDEST DAUGH-
ter's words, Faye was still awake in the early hours of the morning
ruminating over her memories which were melting into impression-
istic scenes of their blossoming bunch of Faultsoms and her brave, but
often faltering, motherhood. Like all young families theirs was a life
that maneuvered through the bedlam of a busy household. But amid
their familiar daily activities, Faye and the children — Constance,
Chance, Charleston, and Chief — learned to *Wonder* around.

At first, more often than not, days at home were mundane, ridic-
ulously uninspired, and unproductive by all accounts. Still, Faye
knew that she had to cultivate a place for *Wonder* to grow in her
children's imaginations, and so it was that she could be overheard by
some nosey neighbor or other, leading a charge that went something
like this:

"Now, children, today we are going to find *Wonder*. Are you ready? Who knows where we might find it . . . and where we might find the door we must open to find our way in? I *do* know that we will never get there if we let our imaginations rot! You see, your imagination is the place where you make space for *Wonder* to open up before you. It begins with beauty and fascination. So, children, look around you and find something gobsmackingly marvelous and clever. Or, better yet, find something terribly average and simple and really look at it, go inside it, examine it, crack its secret code open, and find its hidden design, and then be thankful . . . so thankful that your heart will *explode* inside you. Be thankful that you learned to see in a new way because you have found something *Wonder*-full and then . . . go there!"

So the kids, about whom you will shortly learn a great deal more, followed Faye, toddling off into the world charmed by a little wisp of something that caught their fancy or launching out with great anticipation into cities, woods, lakes, puddles, sand dunes, attics, libraries, old-folks' homes, grocery stores, or even math problems, piano lessons, and chores . . . searching for portals into *Wonderland*.

It would be most satisfying to report that the Faultsom offspring embraced these *Wonder*-seeking excursions without resistance, like the blessed angels we all hope kids will be, but far too often they went about their days with quite a bit of grumbling and fussing.

Slowly and clumsily, the family waded into the unknown as Faye endeavored to help their children see beyond what was right in front of them in order to look into deeper mysteries and explore the landscapes around them with what they called "presentness" exercises. They were all going to need to be very aware and attentive to find ways into *Wonder* and she knew that these ways were definitely not open to those who recklessly indulged themselves in boredom or numbed themselves out with mindless distraction and purposeless stimulation. So, Faye was a real bulldog about TV and video games — cell phones and texting would have driven her quite mad.

To their dismay, however, Frank and Faye learned that instead of awakening appreciation and awe in their children, "presentness" could often make the Faultsom kids quite crabby and out of sorts, for they couldn't be more observant and aware and not be affected by all that they encountered. When things weren't to their liking they became much more ill-tempered. They sometimes got stuck focusing only on those things that disappointed them. The kids noticed that sad things were more mournful, and scary things more frightening. Hunger pangs became peskier, humidity was stickier, a chilly wind was colder, skinned knees were "stingy-er" and, when they really paid attention, the annoyances they felt, as they crammed their oversized personalities into the family van, were oh, *so* much more irritating.

For what seemed like forever, when Faye tried to help them *Wonder*, the kids were often sour, self-centered, and pretty "stinky" with one another. Being bright and inquisitive children unused to repressing themselves, they could turn any well-intentioned afternoon into a riot of drama and discontent.

During her life review, Faye relived one afternoon that stood out to her. It was back when her oldest, Constance, was around twelve, her twin boys, Chance and Charleston, were about nine, and the baby, Chief, was just a little sprout.

While suffering through one of their mom's latest exploratory schemes, an outdoor "stretching and sketching" activity, the older kids sat on the grass tearing tiny corners from their sketchbooks and creating spitballs to lob at each other while bemoaning their fate.

"I hate when she makes us try to be *deep*. Can't Mom ever just let us be? She always has to try and make stuff happen," Constance groused as she sucked on a blob of paper and watched her mom wander out of sight.

"I know, she gets so into her *Wonder* thing, but I'm just not feelin' it today," Chance, the firebrand, agreed as he spewed an especially soggy wad out of his mouth with a gratifying *thhhuuupp!*

"I justh wanna watch Burbey the Brontothaurus. I mithed the last thow!" little Chief whined as a spitball hit his forehead. He burst into tears and shouts of indignation as the rest of the gang began to lay blame.

Faye came running to squelch the din and was discouraged to discover that even the usually affable twin, Charleston — with his overgrown vocabulary and generally mature outlook — was not making things easier:

"Mother, are you sure you have taken into account all of the constants and variables involved in preparing our activities? Things do not seem to be going as you anticipated. Perhaps you should recalculate our trajectory."

Faye frowned as she recalled the episode. It seemed to her to typify many a failed effort on her part. She probably should have lightened up about a lot of things. Had she pressured her kids too much? Had she forced them to try and imagine? Had her pushy passion killed Constance's? Faye was second-guessing her every parenting choice.

She remembered how frustrated they all felt at the time, and how desperate she was to find a way forward. Frank thought that maybe they needed to ensure that family activities were more enjoyable for their children, so they tried to anticipate each of their little Faultsoms' every need and provide more "positive enrichment" games and enjoyments; in essence, cajoling them into cooperation.

"Now, children," they would say in their most lulling tones, "Mother and Father want to help you to be your best, most-fulfilled, and activated selves. We want to enrich your lives today with positive opportunities to grow. Wouldn't you like to participate with us in this process so we can *all* be successful together?" This just made things much worse.

It didn't take too long for Faye and Frank to realize that the door to *Wonder* was shut tight when their children were caught up in themselves, or when *they*, as parents, focused only on pleasing them. Entertaining the children and satisfying their whims left Constance, Chance, Charleston, and Chief disgruntled and dissatisfied — far from *Wonder's* threshold.

One afternoon in the family van during a particularly discouraging attempt at togetherness and discovery, Faye gave her "thankfulness speech" for the umpteenth time that week. From her own experience she just knew that an attitude of gratitude was essential or they would never find their way into *Wonder*. She felt right then and there that she must be raising the most spoiled and ungrateful kids in the whole world.

"Children you are driving me batty! Can't you just find something to be thankful for instead of whining and bellyaching? Without a huge helping of thankfulness, you will never find the *Wonder* that is waiting for you — for us!" Her lecture did not yield its desired results.

Just as she was about to give up entirely and turn the van around and head for home in retreat, Faye suddenly found herself singing . . . *The Song*. She didn't even know where it came from. It just appeared in her head and demanded to be sung. So she gave it a whirl and sang it for the very first time, shocking her kids into silence. Faye did *not* like to sing.

Nevertheless, sing it she did, and over time, the song grew and grew, as if it had a mind of its own. New verses would flow into Faye's mind and out of her mouth until they began to fill the kids' daily lives and alter their world. But oh, how the kids groaned when they first heard it. During frustrating times together, Faye would croak out her infamous melody much to her kids' dismay. When things were going downhill with them she would contain her own peevishness and begin to sing. Somehow her squeaking, cracking voice would prevail over the din.

"Awwww, NOT, *that* song!" the kids would shriek. "Why does Mom have to go on *and on* singing that *song*"?

Secretly, Faye reveled in their torment as she belted it out with great abandon:

You little rotten scoundrels!
Was it something that you ate?
That made you so uncouth, unkind,
Unable to appreciate —
All that lies before you
In the fabric of your days?
Your attitude is stinky and
You'd better change your ways.

You Potty-Snot Nose Miners,
You are in a sorry state
A lovely day's been served to you
Upon a silver plate.
You'd *rather* lick a dirty floor
Than taste the *yummy* stuff?
It's like that when you are a bore
'Cause nothing's good enough.

You little Rug Rat Sillies,
You're just moments from relief
Or days and days from joy if you keep wallowing in grief.
It will come right back to you
With lots more with crud and trauma,
So turn your attitudes around and
Let's avoid the drama!

You Dastardly Despoilers,
Oh how, I do love you so!
No matter what you say or do,
I simply can't say "no"
To what is *best* for you, *and you*,
Oh even if you hate it.
Give up your nasty, rotten ways
So trouble is abated.

Thankful, Thanky, Thankers
That's just what we need to be
Even for the stuff that stinks
Like trash or rot or pee!
For see, there's always something
That is hidden in our woe,
That can open up a door to *Wonder*—
Where we want to go!

Be Jolly, Jaunty Voy'gers!
Let's avoid a conflagration
As we find our happy hearts
And sing for joy with admiration
Of the many little marvels
That *deserve* our cogitation.
Then the *Wonder* door will open
And we'll leave this desolation!

Faye learned to sing *The Song* with the authority of an imperious major general and a buoyant good humor that she refused to surrender despite her kids' worst behavior. As a result, a most miraculous change began to occur. The children actually learned to stop and give thanks for what they saw and experienced, or else, you see, they would have to listen to more of their mom's crooning. Secretly, *The Song*, with all of its rude impishness, won them over. Begrudgingly, they would begin to snicker, and then murmur and mumble, then speak out, and finally *shout* out the things they were thankful for.

They even learned to give thanks for the stuff that they disliked the most. It was hard work but back then, the usually responsible firstborn, Constance, would lead the way for the rest of the kids, who would eventually join in, much to her parents' relief. It was in these times of appreciation in the most annoying and difficult situations that the family first noticed the atmosphere around them began to change, and they would begin to feel a little inkling of hopeful anticipation.

Over time, they moved from self-absorption, to another kind of absorption which was transforming. Most of the time it began as a drab process of just stopping to look deeply, listen carefully, or serve faithfully. But always, it was a time when they were grateful and thanked heartily in the midst of whatever came their way.

As they continued to do this, there would be magnificent little bursts of "twinkle" interrupting the ordinary. One child or another would follow that twinkly feeling into what seemed to be *Wonder's* entrance hall, and then he or she would sense something extraordinary, or perhaps hear a sound or see something that was curious and beguiling.

These experiences were like puzzle pieces that the Faultsoms laid out on the family's kitchen table. Day by day, across the weeks, and months they spread out the bits of mystery they retrieved and cobbled together a doorway here, a window over there, a crack or crevice buried in plain sight — those longed for portals into *Wonder*.

CHAPTER 5

Wide-Eyed and Wondering

THE FAULTSOM FAMILY WAS MADE UP OF SIX DISTINCTIVE
individuals with energy and personality to spare. Since they were
very different kinds of people, it was in very different ways and at different times that they each reported that they'd sort of left themselves
behind and glimpsed another dimension. Bumbling at the threshold
of transcendence, they attempted to "get their sea legs under themselves" as they waded into the waters of *Wonder*. As one or the other
attempted to describe their experiences, the others would nod their
heads with eagerness, as if the next word or phrase they heard could
unlock their own clarity or bring into their world the reality of the
other realm that was becoming so real to them.

Faye and Frank grew to experience the edges of *Wonder* most
often in the eyes of their kids and in the sounds of their voices —
when they weren't yelling with glass-shattering peels and shrieks,
that is. Often they would find themselves caught up in what touched
their childrens' hearts, and this quickly propelled them back, time

and time again, to the mysterious encounters they had had as kids but didn't dare speak openly of when they were young.

Franklin Farnsworthy Faultsom found that when he championed his wife and his children's sensitive spirits, something in him came alive. He could feel himself growing larger inside as he protected and mentored his children, and in stooping to serve, he often had his most profound sense of *Wonder*'s nearness. He regularly tended to many household chores that needed doing so that Faye could fling her cloak of creativity across the arc of any given day, and his gallant service somehow made space for his own hidden quests. When he was immersed in the rhythmic sameness of a simple household task such as folding the laundry or drying the dishes, a smoky campfire smell would encompass him and he would feel as if he were being summoned to join the counsel of a great tribal leader. Sometimes his eyes would even burn and tear up as if he sat before an open fire in a longhouse speaking with a sacred council about matters of great importance. As he stacked the dishes, noble longings would fill him.

Faye Andoria was a soaring and youthful spirit. She didn't feel truly alive unless she was leaning out over a yawning canyon of possibility. She would often dangle herself past the edge of propriety just enough to be prepared in case a sudden draft of *Wonder* might carry her away on its wings. This was a marvel in and of itself, for Faye was prone to motion sickness and actually had quite a shy side. But that was Faye — jumping into the thick of things no matter what and determined that everyone else should be jumping in as well. Nothing thrilled her more than to catch sight of a beam of insight penetrating one of those little Faultsom's skulls she so intently shepherded. *Wonder* seemed to often follow in her wake, even if she didn't realize it was there.

For the ever spiffy, tucked-in, combed-over, and wire-rimmed twin brother, Charleston Chaucer Faultsom, his first foray into *Wonder*'s vestibule was like moving through a filmy, silky curtain of vanilla pudding that wasn't at all sticky. One day while he was playing his cello, he noticed that a kind of lilt and longing was welling up inside him, and as it did, a little slit appeared in the air around him. This happened several times, but each time the feeling faded and the slit disappeared. Then one day, as he was engrossed in his music and full of thankfulness, the slit opened up and what he called a *knowing* enveloped him in a misty pool of sweetness. With each movement of his bow, it was as if he were rowing a boat, and he moved in and around in a swirl of music, fragrance, and light. He even had the power to change where he was and how fast he moved by what and how he played on his cello. Then the mist evaporated, and he was left back in the family music room with a lovely, lingering melody ringing in his ears and an aloof aroma teasing his nose.

Charleston's somewhat shaggy and obstreperous twin brother, Chance Chandler Faultsom, was catapulted headfirst all the way into *Wonder* one day when he lit the fuse to his homemade stink-bomb chain as he hid under the back deck of the house. Chance lit the fuse and watched with glee and scientific satisfaction as the incendiary stench releasers began to spark and sizzle, emitting their pungent odor. He was filled with appreciation for the laws of chemistry as a whiff of smoke smacked his olfactory nerve and sent a thrill right to the center of his cortex, causing his hair to stand on end — which was not at all unlike its usually unruly state.

Utterly absorbed by the epic stink and chaotic wallop of it all, Chance was oblivious to the dire consequences of his stunt as he was suddenly and completely absorbed in *Wonderment*. The smash-and-crash stimulation of this new world was like a roller coaster, a rocket to the moon, and a bungee jump off a canyon precipice — all at once. He could see and hear the sounds of a kind of elemental fusion that produced an energy source unknown in our world. He understood in an instant how it all worked, although for the life of him, when he returned to earth he couldn't quite describe it.

In the meantime, the family's youngest child, the self-appointed family manager and policeman, Conrad Chamberlain Faultsom, aka Chief, with his frizzy red hair, freckles, and toothless grin, discovered Chance's hiding place when he figured out that the cause of the chaos in the family's backyard was coming from under the deck. Sure enough, when Chief crawled underneath the structure, there was Chance, wide-eyed and transfixed. Chief poked at him and breathlessly exclaimed,

"Chancey . . . .you willy did it thith time! Ma is cwazy mad and you betta come up wight now! You betta, or I'll tell her where you are hidin'!"

Chief continued to poke and prod, but there was no getting Chance, whose pupils were dilated and whose mouth was hanging open, to respond. He sat there staring into space sort of

whimpering, until all at once he rasped out loud, "This is so cool! This is SO coooooollllll!"

Well, that was enough for Chief, who figured Chance was caught up in *Wonder*. Naturally, the little boss simply would *not* be left out of anything noteworthy that either of his older brothers got into, so he turned to look at what had captured Chance' attention, screwed up his little "believer," and somehow followed his big brother *all the way* into *Wonder* on the fumes of those old stink bombs.

When Chance and Chief were finally plopped back into the aftermath of the stink-bomb experiment in the Faultsom backyard, the rest of the family was too upset to listen to the excited reports of their time away in *Wonder*. This event was the perilous climax to a season when everyone was crossing into *Wonder* more and more.

Everyone, except Constance.

CHAPTER 6

ᗶLeft Out

WILLOWY, BROWN-EYED CONSTANCE CALANTHA FAULTSOM, with her perfectly coiffed ponytail of thick dark hair and square spectacles, had always been in the center of everything that unfolded in the Faultsom Family. As the oldest child she was the first to be favored and delighted in, and soon became the first responder to the "four-alarm fires" set by her younger brothers and their floppy hound dog, Cornelius.

Through her growing-up years, Constance had had her own *Wonderamas* along the way, but they seemed to her to be nothing as special as those experienced by her other family members. With grave sincerity she worked hard to be attentive to all that happened around her so that she might be able to find her own ways into *Wonder World* as frequently and as fluidly as the others seemed to, but she always felt that she came up short somehow.

As her frustrations simmered into fears, she began to ask herself why her parents so were intense about this whole *Wonder* thing. Why couldn't her mom, in particular, just let them — let *her* — be?

Over time Constance began to stiffen under a growing weight of expectation. The more Faye pressed onward in her quest to make *Wonder* real for the family, the more Constance felt pressured and deficient in some way.

She did her best to be a good sport when others reported the sights, sounds, and smells of this new dimension, which often seemed distant from her. Dutifully Constance would take up the slack and keep things in the "real world" running smoothly when the little kids were a handful or when school and chores were interrupted by the others' jaunts into the netherlands of the extraordinary. Frank and Faye could always count on Constance to hold down the fort when things went wonky or when *Wondering* interrupted their normalcy.

The Faultsoms' eldest did have a deep sense of the realness of *Wonder*, and harbored a space inside her that was filled with hope and possibility about it. Constance reveled in the snippets and anecdotes her family members shared about the feelings, images, textures, and revelations they, to one degree or another, experienced on *Wonder's* outskirts. But why did she feel more and more like she was on the outside looking in?

Constance felt *her* experiences were a drip here and a drop there compared to the more detailed and multilayered tales of her family members. Their stories created a longing in her for more than she encountered, and somehow this made her feel increasingly left out. This longing grew into a wistful melancholy that became a kind of *wishyness* that began to take the place of any *real* hope of ever being fully encompassed in true *Wonder.*

"Mom, I believe. I really do believe. I look, I watch, I wait, and I AM thankful, Mom, I really am. So why doesn't it happen to me the way it happens for Chance and Charleston, or even Chief? All of you are going places I can't seem to get to and you know things I just don't seem to know."

"Okay, but tell me what you *do* know, Constance," Faye would ask.

"Well, I know that you all come back different when you get near *Wonder.* I know that what you learn, you can't get from just the everyday world. I know that what you say makes sense of *this* world, somehow. I know that you love me and that you wouldn't lie to me, but I also know that there seems to be a wall that I can't get over, and the more I try, the higher and thicker it feels, and Mom . . . I'm afraid."

"What are you afraid of?" Faye worried out loud.

Then came the troubled response.

"I'm afraid that you will all go somewhere that I can't *ever* get to."

Faye grew anxious as she watched Constance's growing struggle and redoubled her efforts to help her daughter forge a way through it. She wandered around her daughter's sensitive boundaries, sometimes treading carelessly upon sacred spaces she had not yet discerned in her daughter's heart. Constance often felt pressured and questioned herself all the more.

Frank intuitively understood his daughter better than anyone else, for while Frank had a childlike acceptance of the *Wonder* of it all, he also had to keep his feet on the ground and his head from being caught up in the clouds. Frank didn't overthink things. He had an essentially practical way of *Wondering,* and this was a very good thing for the Faultsoms.

If not for Frank, who knows if his family would ever function in the everyday world. Yes, *Wonder* perhaps *was* the realest of all worlds, in the ultimate sense, but for some reason, they all had to live in the regular world, too. No amount of imagination was going to pay the bills, unless it was the kind of imagination that resulted in more sales and profitability for Peerless Pencil.

Frank shared with great tenderness in the family's excursions and sought his own, but he always made sure his wife and kids stayed tethered to the rock-hard realities of life, as well — gas in the car, food on the table, mortgage, insurance, and taxes paid, chores done, and regular schoolwork completed to his satisfaction. He fiercely treasured his childrens' imaginations and knew that it was essential for his kids to stay out of the Grown-Up Factory. This meant that he must provide a way for Faye to be on deck at all times to captain their daily life instead of pursuing her own career. He also knew something about Constance that no one else knew, including Constance herself.

Frank knew that Constance was actually *more* sensitive to *Wonder*'s call than she realized. He somehow understood that his daughter would carry her deep inner awareness of *Wonder* into the ruthless and practical world around her in a way that perhaps none of his other kids might have to. For Constance secretly carried in her not only the reality of *Wonder* but also possessed a profound awareness of the reality of *Badness*. Of his three children, Her heart was the most perceptive and perhaps the most likely to be broken.

How would such a child manage to thrive in two realms? Frank knew that often those who are the most aware of the darkness around them are the ones who can most easily dry up from the inside out. As his daughter struggled, it pained him because she didn't even know how much of *Wonder* was just a normal part of her being and how the very air she breathed was permeated by the laws and economy of that other dimension, even though it felt distant and inaccessible to her. Sometimes he would sneak into her bedroom at night and hear her murmuring in her sleep. She seemed to be churning inside or wrestling with something or someone. Frank and Faye both knew that *this* child's inner "believer" was utterly awake.

What they didn't know was how much Constance feared she would never measure up to all that *Wonder*. And frankly, could *Wonder* measure up to her expectations? How could a place that was supposed to be so incredible and so beautiful square with the often mundane, ugly, brutal world that she intuitively knew existed somewhere outside of the Faultsom sanctuary? If *Wonder* was real, was it really accessible to her and what of those outside the Faultsoms' world?

In the dim, lonely hours of that long night following Constance's bitter disclosure, Faye's brooding was accompanied by Cornelius and Frank with their snuffling and snoring. She shoved the luxuriating hound dog off of her side of the futon and gave her husband a brief but furious jiggle. This momentarily put a stop to his buzz-sawing while she continued her meanderings through the ups and downs, ins and outs, of *Wondering* that unfolded in and around each of the Faultsoms through those early years.

It had been a time filled with excitement, misadventures, and mistakes, complete with its share of worries. Recalling sweet moments of laughter and grace in the midst of it all, Faye smiled through the tears. This respite from her heavy-heartedness faded quickly, however, as she returned to her concern over the darkness she had last seen in Constance's eyes.

It was then that painful flashes from a quite dreadful time in the life of the Faultsom family invaded Faye's consciousness. Filled with trepidation, but driven by the need to understand her daughter's heart, she courageously peered around the corner of her defenses and into a darker corridor of the past that she knew she must walk down again.

Cautiously, she approached a door that was tightly shut and cracked it open to reveal a space full of foreboding. As she entered reluctantly, she was transported back to a time when the familiar and safe fabric of the Faultsom family life was poised to unravel.

CHAPTER 7

Jeopardy in June

"BEWARE! BE ON ALERT!! A THREAT ISSSS EMERGING. THERE are thossseee who have sssslipped through our fortificationssss. They must be ressssstrained. Their little onesss believe! We must wait and watch for an opportunity to contain them! We will capitalizzzze on their weaknesssssessss . . ."

⋖⋖⋖⋖⋖⋖⋖⋖

Like any young parents, Faye and Frank, were thoroughly occupied with raising their kids, paying bills, running errands, etc., as well as trying to be as respectable as possible which was no easy task considering their unusual circumstances. Unbeknownst to them, they were in a terribly precarious situation, for you will remember that it was a rare person during this era who did not follow in lock step, at least outwardly, with society's skeptical conformity and intolerance of anything truly mysterious or extraordinary. It was risky to question The Prescribed Order (The PO) and practically scandalous for parents not to send their children to a local "Grown-Up Factory."

Their neighbors already thought the Faultsoms were quite strange and were bewildered by the riotous curiosity, energy, and enthusiasm that generally characterized the family wherever they went. Over time, folks in the neighborhood got somewhat used to the Faultsoms. Some even grew to like the family, while others merely tolerated them.

When the officials at the local GUPF were informed that Constance, Charleston, Chance, and Chief were not going to be registered at the facility, they were quite suspicious, to say the least. The Faultsoms' idiosyncrasies raised concerns and furrowed many a brow within the institution. Despite this, they were somewhat limited in what they could do to save the Faultsom children from the perils of their parents' unorthodox methods. Unless, that is, they could prove the children were in some sort of danger. Thus, the officials at The GUPF had been watching the Faultsom family very closely for years to see if they might need to intervene and place the children in a more appropriate environment for their social growth and life-skills development.

In other words, if the Faultsoms could be proved unworthy parents in some way, their children could be forced to attend The GUPF, or possibly even be removed from the Faultsom home. As it turned out, what Faye had planned as a lovely community service and an enrichment opportunity for the kids became the very means by which they were brought under the intense scrutiny of The GUPF facilitators.

It all started when Faye, who had a passion for birds, wanted the kids to learn more about them. She regularly endeavored to bring learning to life with hands-on activities of all sorts. To this end, she would take the kids on bird-watching outings to the local park and zoo, as well as into their own jungle of a backyard. She and Frank dreamed about taking the kids on a birders' safari to the Amazon rainforest to see exotic species in their habitats. This, however, was an unlikely eventuality given the paltry salary Frank received from his labors at Peerless Pencil. Unless their fortunes shifted miraculously, the family would need to find other ways to explore the bird world. It was at this time that Faye met Ms. Imperia Beasley, president of the Busy Birders Ornithology Club.

"Ornithology," Faye explained to the children, "is a branch of zoology, which is all about the study of birds and The Busy Birders study birds like nobody's business."

Indeed they did. They watched birds, sketched birds, and fed birds. They investigated indigenous bird behaviors and habitats, and when birds were in distress, they rescued them. So Faye and the kids volunteered to help the "Busy B's" raise money, which they hoped would also help them build bridges to the community. Most thrilling of all, the family had volunteered to help take care of the birds that were rescued. This activity was very much anticipated by the kids, particularly seven-year-old Chief.

"Mama! Do I get to twain the birdths we help?" quizzed, Chief.

"Nah, you're too little, Freckle Fart. You get to clean the cages," interrupted twelve-year-old Chance with his inimitable way of setting things on fire just to watch them burn.

"I am NOT too little! I am almost theven! Mama, Chance thays I can't twain the birdths! But I will, I will!"

"Cheese whiz, Chance and Chief — chill out!" fifteen-year-old Constance pleaded as Chance continued to prod Chief, who erupted into tears.

At this point the family's other twelve-year-old twin, Charleston, with his usual annoyingly reasonable know-it-all-ness, offered his advice.

"Chance, it would be to everyone's best advantage if you would refrain from provoking our younger sibling,"

"Who died and made you Gumby?" Chance retorted.

"I think you may be referring to *Ghandi*, who just happened to be a famous leader from India, world-renowned for his commitment to peaceful negotiations," Charleston corrected, even as Chance continued to stir things up.

"Ah, put a sock in it, Encyclopedia Brown. You think you're so smart. You're always taking up for Chief, even when he's being a pain in the butt-ox."

"Chancer! Whhhyyyy do you find it necessary to continually inflame things?" Faye cried out in exasperation, just as the kids jumped into a free-for-all of the Blame Game.

Before she lost her temper entirely, Faye began to hum to herself and then to mischievously chant The Song:

> You little rotten scoundrels!
> Was it something that you ate
> That made you so uncouth, unkind?
> Unable to appreciate —
> All that lies before you
> In the fabric of your days?
> Your attitude is stinky and
> You'd better change your ways!

She continued squeaking through the verses, getting louder until she made herself giggle.

> You little Rug Rat Sillies
> You're just moments from relief
> Or days and days from happiness
> 'f you keep giving me your grief.
> I can give it back again
> And wrap it in some trauma,
> So turn your attitudes around and
> Let's avoid the drama.

Three of the kids began to sing and chortle along with their mom, until a bit of sanity was restored, and they were actually feeling their spirits lighten. There *was* something almost magical about that song; it always changed things for everyone — except, in this case, for Chance, who steadfastly staked out his claim to a foul and rebellious mood due to the fact that he earned himself double chores for the week because of his cantankerous behavior.

Ah, yes, it was just another normal morning in the Faultsom home, as the family prepared to host a late June garden party fundraiser for the ornithology ladies. Faye reminded the kids to be on their very best behavior, as The Busy B's would be bringing their most prestigious guests and biggest donors to the Faultsoms' overgrown backyard haven with its flowering plants and bushes, then in peak bloom and attracting many interesting local birds. It was the Faultsoms' chance to demonstrate to the community that they weren't so terribly strange.

It should have been a lovely day. But then, there was Chance, quite perturbed by his lengthened list of chores; very annoyed by the squawking bird ladies who were invading his yard and longing to immerse himself in his new science project on chemical chain-reactions. *And* then, there was Ms. Imperia Beasley, president of The Busy Birders, who, as it would turn out, was *also* the director of the local Grown-Up Factory.

The stage was set for trouble.

CHAPTER 8

The Unexpected Unraveling

THE AFTERNOON STARTED OUT WITH PROMISE. IT WAS A day adorned with a joyous array of chirping birds, extravagant displays of color, and thirsty bumble bees that were staggering from flower to flower sucking in the luscious nectar. The Faultsoms' frenzy of a garden was resplendent, glowing with sunlight and speckled here and there with pools of shade. The breeze carried hints of honeysuckle and jasmine.

Faye and The Busy B's were welcoming guests, and Constance was handing out their mom's famous lavender lemonade, chocolate chip meringues, and almond butter crisscross cookies, as Charleston filled the air with cello music while visitors drifted around the garden reveling in summer's glorious exhibitionism. Chance and Chief were nowhere to be found.

Peppering Faye with questions about the plants in her garden that best attracted area birds and butterflies, The Busy B's and company eagerly slurped up her lemonade. Faye was attempting to fill glasses and answer queries when she noticed that Cornelius needed to be secured. The birders, waltzing around with their goodie-filled plates, were just too much temptation for the family's impetuous hound dog to resist. He had already slobbered up a few unattended almond butter cookies and was sniffing around for more. Faye scanned the yard for help and found none. When she saw Cornelius make another dash toward one of her guest's plates, Faye caught Constance's eye just as her daughter headed out of the back door with a fresh plate of cookies. Faye shot her that "Help me!" look — receiving the "Why does it always have to be me?" look in return.

"Where are Chance and Chief??" Faye wondered irritatedly, as she stepped up onto the deck, scouting the terrain to see if she could spot the missing brothers of the host family.

Just then, she heard a sinister, frizzling, popping sound underneath the deck, followed by a putrid odor rising amidst strands of smoke that filtered up through the wood planks beneath her. The hissing sounds and flashes increased as the deck area was engulfed in smoke and stink, which floated out into the yard on the otherwise welcome summer breeze.

With his sizeable stash of sparklers, rubber bands, and hair collected from the family hair brushes over many months, Chance had managed to a create a linking chain of smoky stink bombs that went off every ten seconds or so until the backyard party was in a shambles. In his mind, this was just another science experiment of the sort his folks had largely encouraged.

"How could something this ingenious be anything but a great idea?" he had rationalized, as he crouched under the deck and struck his first match.

In his heart of hearts Chance knew his darker side was at work in this prank, but having ignored the inner warning voice he jumped into his dubious experiment with both feet. You will remember that moments after Chance lit the fuse, Chief discovered his brother's hiding place and was soon up to his eyeballs in the experiment as well. This stunt, of course, had been the catalyst for their explosive launch headlong into *Wonder*, one right after the other!

It all happened just as Ms. Imperia Beasley had begun to address The Busy Birders (who were assembling around the Faultsoms' deck to bestow their biggest honor upon their largest donor) that smoke and stink invaded the yard.

"Members of The Busy Birders and our esteemed guests we are so thrilled to have you here for the highlight of our Busy Birder calendar of events . . . ," Ms. Beasley intoned.

The bird ladies shrieked as Cornelius began to howl, running back and forth and knocking several of them over, along with a number of chairs and the table upon which the Birders' cherished stuffed-bird collection that had been placed.

Up on the deck, Faye had the best vantage point from which to see the whole unruly wreck unfold, and who should be right next to her in the very center of the cloudy stench? Ms. Imperia Beasley herself! The short, round, and positively pompous president of The Busy B's, with her piercing gaze and pointy nose, was humiliated in front of her most honored guests.

"Friends, ladies, please! Pu—leeze calm down! All will be well . . . " she shouted as she shot Faye a sulfurous glance.

As her blood pressure hit the roof, Faye sprinted around the yard trying to calm everyone down while the introverted and self-possessed Charleston withdrew from the havoc to protect his cello from damage. Since Chance and Chief were missing in action, it fell, as always, upon Constance to moderate the mess and confusion.

"Constance! *Do* Something!" Faye pleaded with her oldest child as if it were all her fault.

Once again Constance would take the heat for not keeping her brothers in check. Mom had made it crystal clear that the family needed to communicate an air of normalcy to their guests and now her daughter was sure she would be held responsible for the turmoil.

"How unfair could life be?" Constance sizzled inside as she began to cough from the smoke and stink. "*I always* listen to what they say, *I always* do what they ask me to do, and *I* help, and *I* always try, *so hard* but the boys get away with murder!"

It was true; Constance could see what the other kids couldn't see — how things around her worked and how much Mom and Dad needed her help and relied upon her. But why was it *her* fault that things had gone so terribly wrong that afternoon?

Just then, Mr. Grover Gooseman, the planned recipient of The Busy Birders' *Gold Medal Giver* award, keeled over and passed out from inhaling the noxious fumes, only to awaken a few minutes later, splashed with lavender lemonade, splattered with bird poop from the freaked-out feathered friends above him in the branches, *and* surrounded by hysterical lady birders who were clucking and squawking like a flock of panicked poultry.

As Mr. Gooseman was regaining consciousness, Chance, holding part of a spent fuse, emerged from under the deck with Chief. Both of the boys stood in front of Faye and her guests, utterly disheveled, reeking like rotten eggs, and shouting with glee.

"Mom, we were there! We did it! We did it, Mom!"

This was terribly incriminating, to say the very least. Chance and Chief looked for all the world as if they were bragging about having maliciously sabotaged the party, when, in truth, they were exalting over their entrance into *Wonder*!

It was then that the smoldering suspicions Ms. Beasley had harbored about the dangerously unconventional Faultsom family were ignited into flame. With her eyes watering and her voice quivering with fury she sputtered at Faye:

"Mrs. Faultsom, I came here open-minded about your irregular family life and very odd educational choices in good faith, offering your children an opportunity to make up for their lack of social normalization. With open arms the members of The Busy Birders welcomed you into our community only to be terrorized by your out-of-control children. As the director of the Dumble Street Center for Child Development and Life Preparation, it is clear to me that your family is unstable, and your children are at risk."

She took a breath and, with a sudden look of triumph, added, "You will be hearing from The Child Developmental Well-Being and Life Skills Assessment Committee, of which I am the head, as soon as

we have fully investigated your family life and determined the state
of your childrens' welfare. We may very well need to intervene with
a plan to ensure the social sensitivity and developmental stability of
your children."

Having risen to a dangerous high due to the catastrophic events
that had just unfolded, Faye's blood pressure suddenly dropped precipitously. She felt a cold chill run down her spine as she took in Ms.
Beasley's words. All at once she was faint and dizzy and her knees
became rubbery under her. This was bad, *very bad*.

Faye did her best to apologize and offer assistance to Ms. Beasley
and her dazed and disoriented guests, feeling the sting of each fiery
look directed at her. By the time the last of the them had finally dis-
persed, a strange sense of impending doom was closing in on Faye
and the kids.

Constance, Chance, Charleston, and Chief had never seen their
mother like this before. Mom hadn't even yelled at anyone — not
even at Chance! She just wandered robotically around the yard in
anxious silence.

"Why is this situation so unusually awful?" the kids asked each other. Hadn't they gotten into worse scrapes on any number of their ill-fated family explorations?

"Remember a couple of years ago, when we visited that mortuary on the way home from the library?" Constance recalled.

"Oh yeah! We sneaked into that funeral home so we could examine an authentic cadaver. We were reading about anatomy and life cycles." Charleston reflected.

"Yeah, when no one was in the room, we got up real close to the open casket and saw that corpse . . . and Chiefy pried the dead guy's eyelid open! What a dope!" Chance carried the story forward with glee.

"Guyths, I juthst wanted to thee if he wath thleeping!" Chief quickly justified himself.

"Unfortunately, the dead gentleman's wife came in right about then and became quite agitated when she saw what happened to his face." Charleston continued.

"Yeah, when she bent down to look at him, she screamed 'cause he looked like he was winking at her," Chance cheered himself with this memory.

"Man, we got in such big trouble! Mom and Dad were upset for days," Constance added, recalling her lack of judgment that afternoon. It was not a good idea to take her brothers into the mortuary in the first place. "But things had somehow settled down even after that mess," she reflected, thinking about how they had all gathered on their parents' oversized and lumpy futon that night to debrief.

Sprawling across the bed and brawling over who owned how much of its real estate, things were in "full Faultsom swing" when Frank, with his sternest fatherly demeanor, issued his rulings to the guilty Faultsom gang. As was expected, the kids were sentenced to hard labor around the house for several weeks due to the funeral fiasco, but even those dire consequences were suddenly remediated by an outbreak of peeling laughter when Chief tearfully apologized for "winking the dead guy" in the coffin.

Surely the garden-party episode couldn't have been as bad as the mortuary mess, the kids reasoned among themselves. After all, this time Chance and Chief had gotten *all the way into Wonder*! They had both actually been there! Wasn't that what they had all been hoping for? How exciting!

The kids' excitement, however, was quickly overwhelmed by a sense of growing apprehension. Without understanding why, none of them could shake the feeling that things would never be the same again and this was not a good thing — not a good thing at all.

CHAPTER 9

It Couldn't Be True

"AH HAAA! WE WILL HAVE THEIR SSSSPAWN AT LASSST!"

"The Court hereby orders that decision-making authority over the education of Constance, Charleston, Chance, and Chief Faultsom be awarded to the State. They will be placed in separate temporary facilities until they can each complete the Social Re-alignment Program."

The words were like a slab of granite slamming down on top of a cold dark hole inside of which Faye and Frank were trapped with no way to get out. They simply could not believe it was true, but it was true.

In the months that had followed the horrid Busy Birders' garden-party debacle, investigators from The GUPF invaded the Faultsom home and uncovered the extent of the family's "dangerous" beliefs and practices. The investigators reported back to the Developmental Well-Being and Life Skills Assessment Committee (The DoWLSAC) and the committee along with the factory facilitators determined that the free-flowing, curiosity-driven educational style of the family was wholly inadequate in preparing the Faultsom children for real-world workforce demands and relationships. Furthermore, the committee was horrified by the otherworldly and imaginative experiences that Faye and Frank Faultsom had fostered in their children.

The family's commitment to their belief in *Wonder* was far worse than Ms. Beasley could have possibly guessed. She was so alarmed by it that she did everything in her considerable power to see to it that the authorities acted to remove Constance, Charleston, Chance, and Chief from their parents' custody and their beloved Dumble Street oasis, for a process of realignment.

As the investigation unfolded through the weeks that ensued, the Faultsom family became increasingly paralyzed with worry, especially when they realized that no amount of common sense, evidence of the kids' growing intellectual and creative abilities, legal representation, or heartfelt appeals seemed to make a difference. Even the string-pulling attempted by Frank's influential father seemed to do no good. The facilitators of The GUPF were determined to make an example of the Faultsoms. Daring to teach children to think and act differently from that which the factory facilitators considered "developmentally desirable," simply would not be tolerated. The Prescribed Order must be adhered to.

To make matters worse, the family's portals into *Wonder* seemed to be shut up, barred, and locked tight. After that fateful summer day, no one in the Faultsom family seemed willing or able to enter in.

Chance was totally guilt-ridden that his antics had been the cause of the upheaval. He had been the one who lit the fuse and everyone had gotten burnt because of it. Chance never wanted to go anywhere near *Wonder* — ever again.

Charleston had gone deep inside himself to ponder everything with an intensity that shocked even those closest to him. Who knew when he would come up for air? He and Chief still believed, but were deeply shaken and most disheartened to find that the doors into their beloved *Wonder*, which had once been available to them, seemed to have disappeared. They felt locked out and abandoned to their own threatening world.

For Constance this was just another example of how she didn't "do enough." Of course she was responsible for the fact that things had gotten out of hand. If only she wouldn't have copped that attitude just when Mom needed her help at the party. If only she would have tried harder to help. Constance's heart and imagination were hit hard and severely wounded. As things deteriorated for the family, her worst fears seemed to be realized. Because of their belief in *Wonder*, she really *was* going to be separated from the people she loved more than life itself. She grew angry and resentful.

It wasn't long before Faye and Frank began to second-guess their parenting decisions and think that perhaps they had been totally unhinged to believe in *Wonder*. Perhaps they had simply been delusional all along. Now they were responsible for the fact that their kids were scrutinized and harassed for their beliefs. So it was that a cold, stony fear settled over the family and shut down their imaginations.

It was the darkest of dark days for the family when The State's Well-Being Officers (The WBOs) arrived to take the children off to their separate locations for a period of social re-grounding and realignment. Frank and Faye stood by helplessly that afternoon as the kids' belongings were loaded up and Constance, Charleston, Chance, and Chief were directed toward the waiting cars.

One by one the Faultsoms began to sob as they clung to each other in a final embrace. Their dreams had been crushed and their family was broken. All for the sake of their strange belief in a place no one could prove even existed at all. Faye and Frank felt a smothering shame and fear. They had made a terrible mistake. Their imaginings had ultimately caused their children nothing but heartache.

"Come along now, kids," the head WBO interrupted, as his deputies began to peel the family from each other's arms. "It's time to go. We are taking you to a stable place where you will learn about how things work in the real world and you will be liberated from all of this ridiculous hocus-pocus you've been brainwashed to believe in . . ."

That was it for Chief.

Something broke loose and roared out of him. Just at the moment, when every one of them thought they could never dare to imagine anything *Wonderful* again, he screamed out:

"I – WILL – ALWAYTHS BELIEVE! I don't care what anyone thays! You cannot take my imaginathon away from me! And ya' know what? No matter what happenths, I AM THANKFUL! I am thankful for my mom and my dad who taught me to imagine. I am thankful for *Wonder* and I am even thankful for all of thith rotten thuff, becauth *Wonder* ith even *more real* than *any* of thith nonthenth . . . I know, because *I've* been there! AND *I've* met The Gate Keeper and he is the mothst realethst perthon there ith!"

The family reeled at this revelation. This was something he had never told them. *Chief had actually met someone in Wonder!* As it turned out, the littlest Faultsom had felt so ashamed that he was associated with the stink-bomb stunt that he had doubted his experiences and had chosen not to disclose his contact with this "Gate Keeper." But now, Chief was shouting it from the rooftops and they were all in shock. Could *Wonder* really be real after all?

Each Faultsom froze to take this in as Chief burst out singing, at the top of his lungs:

Be Jolly, Jaunty Voy'gers!
And we'll avoid a conflagrathion
Ath we find our happy hearths
And thing for joy with admirathon
For the many little marvelth
That *detherve* our cogitathon.
Then the *Wonder* door will open
And we'll leave thith desolathon!

This final verse of "The Thong," as Chief called it, suddenly rose up in each of them, and every family member began to sing it — over and over. And, as if that weren't enough of a surprise, they all began to shout out what they were thankful for, even though they were in the middle of the most dreadful and distressing situation they had ever faced. A jumble of Faultsom voices created a chorus of thanksgiving.

"I'm thankful for all the love in our family!"

"I'm thankful for all of our crazy adventures!"

"Thank you, Mom and Dad, for helping us learn to imagine and believe in things that are so . . . so . . . *amazing*!"

"Hey, that makes *us amazing* — we are an *amazing family* . . . I'm thankful for that!"

"Thank you, Dad and Mom, for letting us be different!"

"I'm thankful for how weird and thilly we are!"

"*I'm* thankful that Chance hasn't blown us all up yet!"

"Yeah, and I'm thankful that Chief isn't really the boss, though he thinks he is!!"

"I even apprethiate Charlie's mopey ole cello muthic!"

"Well, I'm thankful that I don't have to be as perfect as Constance is — *not*!"

"I'm thankful that I have four outrageous and ingenious children and the most original, and adventurous wife on the planet!" Dad shouted out followed by Mom.

"And I'm thankful for you, Frank. If it weren't for you, well, we'd be . . . lost . . . "

And so, there they were on Dumble Street, crying and laughing and singing and shouting together as if their lives depended upon it, for indeed they *did* depend on it. Meanwhile, as all this was going on, The WBOs were stunned and utterly unable to move.

Cornelius, the Faultsom hound dog, began barking wildly and running back and forth between the family members because something exceedingly weird was happening and all The WBO's could do was just stand there and gape. For you see, as the Faultsoms continued to erupt with expressions of thanksgiving and song, they also began to fade from view as if they were changing substance! They were thinning out, while at the same time, they were becoming kind of glowy. Then all at once, they disappeared completely! Cornelius, the head WBO and his squad stood by utterly dumbfounded, staring at an empty sidewalk, with bits and pieces of *The Thong* echoing off in the distance.

"The *Won-won-won-der* doooor . . . o-pen — nnn . . ."

"Leave thissss . . . de- so- lay- shun — shun — shun-nnnnn . . ."

CHAPTER 10

The Gate Keeper

"WELL, WELCOME, MR. AND MRS. AMAZING. WELCOME TO you and your family of Amazelings!"

They had just been whooshed through a cool, refreshing mist and then plopped under a warm shower of sparkling . . . what was it? Apple cider? Was that what it was? It wasn't sticky but, yes, they were drenched in a sweet, fragrance like that of ripe, just-picked apples. They stood there immersed in the aroma and bathed in "happy" — that's the only word for it — *happy* light.

Standing in front of them was a portly little person dressed in a uniform that suggested a rank of high level and importance and yet he had a whimsical quality as well. It was decorated with strips of various widths and colors that reminded Frank of military ribbons. But on this man's uniform, the stripes went up and down across the front of the jacket, rather than across his chest. The jacket also sported big, spiffy buttons and gained its regal air from very fine gold epaulets which rested on its the shoulders. It was further adorned with a wide black belt that circumnavigated the man's sizeable tummy, fastening itself with an oversized and ornate golden belt-buckle. The ensemble was topped off by a most unusual helmet covered in a strange hodge-podge of shapes that fit together all over it like puzzle pieces. This, along with a marvelous, munificent white mustache, accentuated the little gentleman's chubby, reddish face and merry eyes.

"Well, you've certainly gotten yourselves into quite a pelick . . . or kilclep," he scratched his head . . . "Or did I mean "pickle? Oh," he muttered to himself, "I can never quite keep track of all the silly little sayings and funny sounding words in your world. It's so sendoriat-ing, oh no, that's not it . . . ahhh, dis—orient—ing . . . ah yes . . . that's it! Any hoo, you folks really did make quite an entrance and just when I thought you'd NEVER get here. Transmissions from Lumbde Lane . . . or is it *Dumble Street* . . . Yes, that's it, transmissions from Dumble Street have been shut down for some time."

They were all breathing in the lovely cider fragrance and adjust-ing to the shock of their very "sendoriating" experience, when he wiggled his distinguished mustache, sniffed the air with his bulbous red nose, and declared:

"Glad we washed all of that nasty unbelieving and afraidness smell off of you. No one gets in here with the stench of *that* on them. My name is Mr. Keeze and I can pretty much unlock anything around here if you really want to get in — once you've actually gotten here, that is."

"Thath's him! Thath's him," Chief whispered breathlessly as he yanked on his parents' clothing. "Thath's the man I met when I wath here with Chanth before!"

"Well, sir, ah Mr. Keeze," stuttered Frank as he brushed away Chief's pawing hands and struggled to gain composure. "I—I am Frank Faultsom and this is my wife, Faye, and our children."

"Yes, of course you are! Helloooo, Mr. Chief! So good to see you here again. We said a brief how-do-you-do when you and your brother burst through our doorway once not so long ago . . . "

Chief's chest puffed out in sudden self-importance as Mr. Keeze grabbed his hand and vigorously shook it.

"Ah, sir, where *exactly* are we?" Frank ventured.

"Why *Erdwon* . . . of course!" replied Mr. Keeze, as he gazed incredulously at them.

"Erdwon?? Where is that??" Frank asked. The family was quite puzzled by this.

"Erwon, did I say Erdwon . . . ? Why, I meant . . . *Wonder*."

"*Wonder*?! This is it?" Frank exclaimed in shock.

"This is it?" Constance asked.

"We are all really here?" the kids all cried out in excited whispers.

"Well, this isn't it, entirely. There are zillcadsions of places that you can go in *Wonder*." They looked at him in confusion.

"No, that's not it — hmmm . . . ah! There are *scadzillions* of places here — lots and *lots* of them! More than you could visit in a forever, but based on what I know about you folks, it makes sense that you'd wind up here. This is a good place to go when you are dustflered . . . ah, flustered about the realness and true-ness and *The All of it All*."

"I take it from the smells you brought with you that you folks are pretty pukenash right now . . . oh dear . . . my, my, *shaken-up*, that is . . . about the basics. And so we shall begin to sort that out."

They were all so shocked and thrilled to be out of trouble and so overwhelmed by the sight of Mr. Keeze (The Gate Keeper himself!) that they were as speechless as the Faultsoms could ever be, though their minds were bursting with hundreds of questions.

"Well, don't just stand there looking like something the drat cagged in . . . ah, *cat dragged in* . . . We've got some serious *Wondering* around to do. *Xartief* has given me instructions to guide you around these parts and put some things to rights. We mustn't delay."

"*Xartief*? Who could that possibly be?" they asked themselves but, before they could even begin to ponder this, Mr. Keeze reached his little fat fingers up and onto his helmet and fumbled around, apparently trying to feel his way about its unusual surface. He began to pull out puzzle piece things from the helmet. One by one, he extracted them and when, upon inspection, he found them not to be what he was looking for, he would let the pieces go in midair and they would each whiz back into place on his headgear by means of snappy, retractable golden strings. For some reason, the family had the sense that these strange and colorful puzzle pieces were, in fact, fantastic keys. While Mr. Keeze fumbled with his helmet, the Faultsoms stood there in the warm, happy light as the shock of their circumstances faded. They felt better and better as they noticed that the dread they had felt when they stood on Dumble Street was now far away.

"Oh, for the love of tubtunteaper, I just had it here. Did I say "tubtunteaper?" Oh dear, what is a fellow to do with such a strange language as yours? *For the love of . . . peanut butter . . .* I simply don't have anymore time to worry myslef, ah *self . . .* , about the right words.

There's is so much to be seen and done." He continued to fumble around until he found a long, skinny sort of giraffish-shaped thingy that he pulled from his helmet. He squinted with one eye closed, and looked at it carefully. Determining that this was the sought-after item at last, he then escorted the family out of the happy light shower toward a long column of doors. They hadn't noticed the doors before, but there they were, stretching out for an infinity to the right and the left, as if they were looking at a single door reflected back and forth thousands of times between two mirrors.

He walked tentatively toward the line of doors, which were all different from one another and each very curious and grand. He paced up and down in front of the doors for a bit, talking to himself:

"Hmmm, where did I leave that rood, no — it is called a *door*. Ah yes, here it is." Then, pulling the giraffy thing from his helmet by its string, he put it into the one empty spot on the face of the portal he had selected where it fit perfectly. The puzzle piece was indeed a fantastic key, and as soon as the key clicked into place, it zinged back into its spot on Mr. Keeze helmet as all the other "roods" disappeared and the one before them swung wide open. They then found themselves entering what seemed like a long, long hallway that went straight — up.

"Here we go . . . everyone into the Enmast wupay . . . hmm . . . no it's an *up-way*. Come on in now," directed Mr. Keeze.

Not knowing what an "Enmast" was and having no other choices before them — but somehow knowing that Mr. Keeze was a safe guide — they proceeded to squeeze inside the up-way. This they did with the usual Faultsom banter and excitement rising among them, as it sank into each one that they were all safe and sound and all together in the very place they had been longing to gain entrance to for so long.

The door closed behind them.

"Ho there, Enmast, please take us on up." And Enmast, whoever or whatever that was, quivered slightly around them as if to acknowledge the command and then obey. They all began to rise higher and higher as if they were being pulled up the kitchen sink drainpipe by their hair, though it didn't hurt a bit. They jutted gracefully back and forth to the left and right a couple of times as they rose, until they reached the top and were deposited on a platform of sorts next to what might be a wall.

"Here we are, Sir Renath, open up, please!" Again there was a little quiver of respect and acknowledgment, and a path opened for them through the wall and into "Sir Raneth," which was apparently the name of the chamber before them. They entered a long, fairly narrow enclosure that grew narrower and narrower until it reached what almost seemed to be a point on the other end. Inside this elongated cone-shaped space, they noticed a woody moist smell in the atmosphere as they walked forward on a spongy surface between four long, porous tubelike structures that protruded from the wall they had just come through. There were two tubes — one low and one higher — on either side of them. These were parallel to the floor and reached quite far across the length of the room.

"Hello there, Microspangoria — oh bother, that's not quite the right word but it will have to do. Hello there!" Mr. Keeze greeted the tubes with enthusiasm. As he led the Faultsoms along between them, the "Microspangorias" wiggled their own greeting back. He continued, "Tell our friends what you're up to."

At that, the family began to hear vocal sounds, but no other person was talking. The Faultsoms peppered each other with questions and comments as they tried to figure out what they were hearing.

"Hey, cool, did you hear that?" Constance asked.

"Chance, Chief, was that either of you?" Dad inquired.

"Nope, not uth!" Chief answered

"But we are hearing voices!" Faye remarked excitedly.

"Ssshhh!" Frank said.

"Listen!" Constance whispered.

The family heard four distinct voices coming from the four Microspangoria tubes beside them.

"Tap tap tap, tap pe tum, tap tap tap pe tum. We are covered with Tap tap tap, tap pe tum, tap tap tap pe tum," came from one of the tubes over and over again as if it were playing a little hand drum.

"Dip dip dip lo—id dip dip dip lo—id dippy dippy dip dip lo—ids! Inside us there is Dip dip dip lo—id dip dip dip lo—id dippy dippy dip dip lo—ids," a deeper voice intoned in a rich bass sound.

"Phytesporephytesporephytesporephytesporesphyte . . ."

"Ioioioioioioimeioioioioioemeiosisssssssssssssss . . ." came the melodies from the other tubes.

The voices spoke to one another, well, no . . . they vocalized together, creating a melodic rhythm that inspired each of the visitors to tap their toes and sway back and forth slightly to the odd but catchy groove they were hearing.

Charleston found himself humming a little melody over the top of this, and Chief began to stomp his foot as Chance eyed the enclosure for something to beat on like a hadn drum. The others joined in the melody as they felt the force of the rhythm rise around them. It seemed to be building to a conclusion. Which in fact it did, as one by one, starting from the bottom up, the Microspangorias each emitted a tone forming a single chord in harmony. The tubes wavered at different frequencies, but the effect was a four-note chord so full and unified that it vibrated powerfully through them. Every cell in their bodies seemed to hum with an energy that fully awakened their senses. Faye wished she had a sound like this at home with which she could awaken slumberous Constance and Chance, both of whom could easily to hibernate far into any day.

The Faultsoms stood enthralled in the center of the sound as it swelled in and around them until, at last, the tubes all sang one thing together.

"Sporosporosporosporo—pollllllllllennninnnn!"

"Ah, that's the sound of the Dartets . . . no, no that's not it. Ah . . . the *Tetrads*. They have arrived! Yes, the Tetrads!" Mr. Keeze exclaimed.

"Sporosporosporosporopollllllllllennninnnn!" came a hushed whisper from the tubes.

At this point the family realized that inside those peculiar tubes, strange and remarkable developments had been taking place. Now, little woolly balls were becoming visible, covering the tubes as they grew fuzzier by the second. They were sunny-orange fellows who were talking feverishly among themselves as they expanded in size and number to cover the Microspangoria tubes entirely.

"Hey, Ho there, brothers!"

"Here we are!"

"Ever the eager explorers, aren't we?"

"Don't crowd now. Make room — make room for one another," came a riot of voices.

"Ready to go? Ready to go?"

"Can't wait to make the trip!"

"It's the best part about being us . . . except for the fun of deploying and then, of course there's the Downing and Digging!"

"Yes! Indeed!" blathered the fuzzy little chaps.

"My natty little Llopens!" Mr. Keeze cried. "You are the rakish fellows, aren't you? You're quite richepp, ah — *chipper* today, I'd say!" Mr. Keeze was barely able to contain his own amusement and clearly unable to contain theirs, even as they acknowledged him in waves of wee wiggles and quivers.

As the Faultsoms watched in fascination, the "Llopens," as Mr. Keeze called the lint balls, kept multiplying, becoming puffier and fluffier, and more and more yellow, and more and more frenzied as they covered the Microspangoria tubes. When it seemed that not another little fuzzball would fit onto another one of the four tubes, Charleston and Constance began to notice that they were getting itchy all over. It was becoming, well, just plain *torture*. Soon they felt like they would jump out of their skins. Their eyes were irritated and their tear ducts were brimming with water like the crest of the Niagara Falls!

"Mom, my skin is becoming so irritated. It's almost unbearable!" Charleston cried.

"Dad, everything is soooo itchy! My eyes are gushing! What *is* this, ?!!" yelled Constance.

"What's happening? Mom, Dad, help!" They both began to panic and cry, as Faye and Frank tried to help. Just when the kids both thought they'd explode with hysterics from scratching as they burst into typhoons of watery sneezing, the family heard a screeching, rubbery, stretching sound above them that was growing increasingly intense.

Scccrreeeecchhhh! Zzzcchhhhheeeekkkkksh! The sounds were ear-piercing and quite unnerving. The sound was like metal being dragged over concrete. The Faultsoms covered their ears and huddled together as the sounds grew more and more intolerable. At the peak of the screeching, Sir Raneth's chamber ceiling ripped open lengthwise from one end to the other.

Suddenly they were staring up at a brilliant expanse of blue, engulfing them in an awe that almost ripped the air out of their lungs, as they instantly felt like the miniscule specs that, in fact, they were.

"Amazlings! Take hold!" shouted Mr. Keeze, "Grab on to a Llopen . . . we must be off!"

CHAPTER 11

Fuzz in Flight

WITHOUT ANOTHER WORD, MR. KEEZE REACHED OUT TO one of the eager little Llopen frizzies that was closest to him. When he touched it, he disappeared instantly, leaving the Faultsom family quite startled, staring up at an immense swath of blue, surrounded by supercharged Llopens on all sides and wondering what to do next.

"Well, everyone, what now?" Frank puzzled.

"We gotta go. Mr. Keeze ith gone and he thaid we have to be off!" Chief insisted.

"I think he means for us to follow him somehow," Charleston offered, as he wiped his eyes and nose on his sleeve. Both he and Constance were starting to feel less itchy and sneezy now that fresh air was moving around them.

"He told us to grab onto the Llopens — but they are so small and we are so big." Constance added, sniffling.

"It doesn't seem possible, but maybe we should try." Faye suggested.

The family could feel fresh wisps of air blowing around them as the Llopens continued to puff up on all sides. It was a real relief that Charleston and Constance were, indeed, recovering — suddenly immune to whatever it was that had been so terribly vexatious and irritating to them. But, it was clear that the family had a decision to make, and fast! What were they going to do next?

"Come on, let's see what happens when we touch the Llopens!" Chance piped up.

The family agreed hesitantly, but before Frank could give the go-ahead, Chief, wanting to be first to follow Mr. Keeze, reached out to touch a patch of yellow fluff that was on the Microspangoria closest to him. Immediately, he disappeared from sight!

"Hey!! Now thith futhball ith way bigger 'n' me!" he chirped. It was true. Chief had shrunk in size and the Llopen, whose fuzz he had reached out to touch, was enormous.

"Chief! Chief, where are you?" Frank and Faye cried out.

"Wight here, Ma and Pa!" Chief screamed as loud as he could. "I'm wight here . . . look! Wight nexth to you!"

Faye and Frank could hear a teeny little squeaking sound that somehow seemed familiar.

"Hey, that's Chief's voice!" Charleston discerned, with his sensitive musician's ears.

"Yeah, ith's me! Grab a Llopen!" shouted the pip-squeaky voice.

"I guess we'd better do it, guys," Frank ventured apprehensively. "We need to figure out what happened to your little brother and catch up with Mr. Keeze, and I don't see another way to move forward from here."

Constance, Charleston, and Chance, along with Faye and Frank, reached out into the mass of yellow fluff on the Microspangoria tube nearest to them. In doing so, one by one, the Faultsoms popped out of sight, becoming teensy-weensy. The Llopens were now the size of elephants compared to the size of the Faultsoms.

"Oooh, gross . . . this Llopen thing . . . is huge and it's really icky!" Constance squealed.

"Fascinating," Charleston mused. "It seems that we have diminished in size considerably. I, for one, am dwarfed by this creature and it is quite . . . quite viscous. I am holding on to the Llopen, but it appears that, in truth, the Llopen is adhering to me!"

"Yeah, it's sticky! I feel like I'm covered in orange cotton candy!" Chance observed.

"Is everyone here? Is everyone okay?" Frank shouted. Frank himself was shrunken and covered in a gummy yellow substance, but had survived. He could only hope that his family was safe, even though he couldn't see them.

"At last, friends! You've got the hang of it now . . ."

They could just make out the voice of Mr. Keeze as he shouted out to them. "Standby! My fa—vor—ite part of the job this is!"

Just then, the zippy Llopens became all the more wiggly and excitable as anticipation filled the atmosphere. At the same time, Faye and Constance noticed an intoxicating fragrance swirling around them.

"Oh my!" exclaimed Faye . . . this fragrance is . . . heavenly!"

"I've never smelled anything like it before!" Constance marveled. Now they all could smell it.

"Wow, I'm feeling dizzy!" Frank said.

"It's almost overpowering." Charleston stated.

"Trippy!" Chance said as his sucked in more of the sweet smell through his nostrils.

"I jutht want to curl up in thith thmell and float away . . ."

Chief was drifting off. In fact they were all starting to become lightheaded and loopy.

"Now, now, Amazings," Mr. Keeze broke in. "Keep your wits about you. We must be at the ready, for the *Scent has been Sent*." He laughed to himself with no small amount of glee. "Yes, the signal has been released and the Llopinators are coming! They are coming for Tenarc. Crazy for it, pining for it, mad for it, they are! Be alert!"

"Cheeze Whiz, I wish this guy would speak English," Constance muttered to herself. "I have no idea what he is talking about! 'Enmast — Raneth — Microspangoria — Llopens?' So weird! And what the heck is 'Tenarc?!' Now I'm stuck here covered in yellow goo, waiting for some sort of Llopenmonsters or whatever he called them. Accchh!" Constance was most perturbed.

One might suspect that each of the family members shared these feelings, but everything was happening so quickly there wasn't time to sort it all out, much less complain or truly worry. All they knew was that being in *Wonder* consumed their full attention, and now they were infinitesimally small and quite sticky.

Then they heard a very fast *whoop, whoop, whoop, whooping* — a kind of whirring sound, and whatever it was, it was definitely getting louder and closer.

Then came the excited voice of Mr. Keeze shouting at the top of his shrunken-down lungs: "Here they come, my ginazam drenifs, I mean, my amazing friends! Incoming Llopinators ahead!"

From a distance, a growing darkness descended over them and their thoughts were drowned out by a deafening noise. It was as if a cyclone it was about to hit. As it neared, they were thrashed about in powerful gusts of wind.

They caught sight of a gargantuan brownish-black thing flying toward them. There was a flash of yellow overhead as the Faultsoms ducked deep inside their Llopens, hoping to shield themselves from the overwhelming approach of whatever these things were. That is, everyone ducked inside except for Chance who, for all the world, would not have missed the danger and thrill that accompanied their arrival. To him the "Llopinators" were like living helicopters, but then, he was so small compared to their scope and size that it was impossible to get any real sense of what they actually looked like or how they functioned.

The roar of the whirlwind above them began to quiet and they sat buried in their Llopens under the dark cloud of one of the landing Llopinators, peeping out and trying to get a look at who or what it was.

"Why, it's Mistress Bublem Eeb" exclaimed Mr. Keeze. "She's one of my favorite Llopinators. Quite a daly, oh no, I mean, quite a *lady*. Greetings, Mistress Eeb!" "Mistress Eeb" seemed to move her mammoth body as if to offer a nod of response.

As she hovered over them and landed, they could see jointed appendages with razor-sharp edges, which served as her landing gear. These extended down from her body and rested on the Sir Raneth and brushed up against the Microspangoria tubes on which the family sat, pasted to the Llopens.

Suddenly, Llopens everywhere around them began to cheer with abandon, for now many of their peppy, tacky wee selves were sticking to the limbs of the Llopinator and, along with them, stuck the Faultsoms!

"Here we go boys!" the Llopens cried.

"We'll soon be off!"

"Let's hit it!"

"We're on board now!"

The Faultsoms were swimming in the chatter of the Llopens, trying to figure out what they were so excited about, when suddenly the family heard mighty whooshing, slurping noises coming from inside the creature that Mr. Keeze called "Mistress Bublem Eeb." This was intermittently followed by what seemed to them to be the sound of pleasure. Yes, in between the slurping noises they heard a satisfied hum that expressed what they intuitively knew was delight. This was confirmed when they heard Mr. Keeze call out to her.

"That's it, Mistress Eeb, enjoy the Tenarc! I know you relish it so."

The air grew still for a few moments, and then, without warning, the creature to which their Llopens were now affixed took to the sky. Suddenly Mr. Keeze and the Faultsoms, stuck to their Llopens, were whisked away.

"My favorite part of the job — this is!" they heard Mr. Keeze's voice exclaiming,

"Wee! Wee!" Chief squealed.

"This is awesome!" Chance was exploding with excitement.

"Wha-aa! Whooo hoo!" Charleston felt the thrill of the liftoff.

"Wow, we're flying!" Frank was in shock.

Faye was starting to get queasy, "I think I'm going to be sick . . ."

"Whoah . . . This is cool!" Constance called.

It *was* quite a thrill at that. Constance, Charleston, Chance, Chief, Frank, and Faye were treated to the ride of their lives, as the Llopinator, Mistress Bublem Eeb, lifted off and maneuvered quickly from left to right, up and down, swooping and weaving in and out and around massive colorful landscapes that seemed to erupt before them out of nowhere. The creature had an agility and grace apparent to her passengers, even though they were merely microscopic specs caught on her landing gear.

As the family was transported from one destination to another, intoxicating aromas like the one they had experienced just before Mistress Eeb first arrived were billowing around them and filling their senses with pleasure. It seemed to Faye and to Constance that the fragrances were like trails leading the Llopinator-thing to the glorious basins and summits of hues and textures that she made her way in and out of.

Now and again, she would stop and slurp and hum and rejoice. The Faultsoms found themselves enchanted by the gigantic Mistress Eeb, and they felt a strange empathy with her, whatever she might be. Indeed, they discovered they had a capacity to perceive her feelings and even her personality. Years later, when they looked back on their fantastic flight that day, they recounted to one another how Mistress Bublem Eeb seemed to them to be like an endearing child, earnestly absorbed in the joyous business of exploring a backyard on a fine summer's day.

And what a day it was! They could hardly trust their senses. The Faultsoms were flying around spectacular mountains and valleys of the most vivid pinks, purples, golds, and reds. Sometimes they would land right in the middle of a canyon of saturated color and fragrance, and as they did, various troops of Llopens would disembark Mistress Eeb as they stuck themselves to the surface she landed on. Going on their way they would call out to one another:

"It looks like this is where I'll get off, lads . . ."

"And us, too."

"Time to deploy! We're off to Down and Dig!"

"And to Generate!"

"Ho, ho, yes — yes!"

"Generate!"

"Generate, that's just what Xartief has charged us to do!"

"Xartief be extolled!" They would exclaim among themselves.

The Faultsoms overheard the Llopen chatter and tried to make sense of it. They *Wondered* about the Llopens' strange banter and about this "Xartief" they spoke of so exultantly. How odd this word made them feel when they heard it. There was a quickening in their hearts each time it was spoken, but they never had a moment to ponder the feeling. Especially not when they found themselves taking off again and noticing that most of the Llopens nearest to them had been left behind. When Frank saw this, his inner alarm bell began to ring and he began to worry. Were his wife and kids still on board Mistress Eeb?

Desperately he tried to take a roll-call, shouting as loudly as he possibly could:

"Is everyone still on this Eeb thing? Please tell me if you are here!" Frank could barely make out the voices that called back just as they began to take off.

"I'm here, honey," Faye called out.

"Dad! I'm here, it's me Dad."

"Me too . . . !"

"Ith me, Papa!"

Frank heard the responses of his wife and his three sons.

Straight up they whooshed . . . up, up, and away. If they could have heard the screeching, terrified sound coming from below them they would have recognized that it Constance screaming with all her might.

"Dad, I'm down here! Help! Don't leave . . . I'm stuck here — I'm stuck! Don't leave me! Please!"

But Frank could not hear her voice, nor could the other Faultsoms. They were rising up and flying away . . . into the wild blue *Wonder*.

CHAPTER 12

‛Left Behind

ALONE. HER FAMILY WAS GONE AND CONSTANCE WAS ALONE — with a bunch of weird, annoying, overgrown lint balls who would *not* stop chattering and fussing. They reminded Constance of her immature, adolescent brothers at their worst. And if that weren't bad enough, she was covered in their goop on some freakish island of pink, watching her family fly away on a creepy brown monster-copter!

A wave of panic hit her as she stared up at the sky and caught her last glimpse of their Llopinator, Mistress Eeb, flying away. For a brief moment Constance thought there was something familiar about her. What did the creature remind her of? She wasn't sure, but why did that even matter now? Constance was in the strangest crisis imaginable, overwhelmed and terrified. She started to cry.

Rivers of tears flowed from her eyes, releasing the pent up anxiety and sadness she had held inside for months and spilling onto her Llopen, which seemed to lap up her tears instantly. She cried and cried, and the more she cried, the more she moistened the

Llopen, causing it to swell in size around her, making her all the more miserable.

"This is just horrid! My family is gone and I have no idea where I am. How could this happen? Oh, what am I noging do to? NO! What am I *going to do*?" Now she was really frightened, for she was starting to talk like Mr. Keeze and getting her words all fuddled. This really was a mess.

She felt lost, trapped, and icky, and was just about to completely fall apart, when she heard a faint voice coming from not so very far away.

"Now now, Amazeling Constance, do not despair." It was the voice of Mr. Keeze, who had been fully occupied mediating a guffuffle that had broken out among the local Llopens. It seemed they were vying with one another for the opportunity to disembark and determine who got to stay and who should leave with Mistress Eeb.

Constance continued her wailing as Mr. Keeze lobbed words of comfort her way.

"Everything here happens just as it should, but *never* as expected, my dear. What would be the *Wonder* in that? You and I have things explore. Let's get to it, shall we?"

At that, Constance found herself lifted up and out of her Llopen, noticing that her panic and frustration were also lifting as the gooey, globby stuff she was covered in mysteriously melted away. What a relief! But now she was floating down, around, and inside the bright pink landscape upon which Mistress Eeb had left her, and what a refreshing feeling it was! She was lighter than the air on which she was blown about inside the deep yawning cavern below her that sunk precipitously out of sight.

Fascinating sculptures, what seemed like rock formations, and promontories reached out toward her from the walls of the canyon as Constance flitted past them, swirling lower and lower around a vast pipelike central structure that rose up from the bottom of the canyon and grew up and out of the top. In fact, Constance thought that this pole of sorts might have been the supporting shaft under Mistress Eeb's landing pad in the center of the immense pink gorge.

But there was no figuring out all of that now, for during her airy descent, Constance was filled with exhilaration as hues and shapes, light and shadows stimulated and overwhelmed her red puffy eyes. A joyously honeyed fragrance tickled her nose.

"Haaaaaa . . . Heeee! " She heard the childlike squeals of Mr. Keeze rising around her as well.

"Hellooooo there, Lady Lyste, with your terriiiific Timstag on top! Mistress Eeeeb dropped us off upon it!" he shouted to the imposing center pole as he floated around it.

"Fa—vor—ite part of the boj—no *the job* thissss issssss!" He delighted. "Oh the joys of unlocking the *Wo—nnnn—dddder* of it all!"

"Oh Mr. Keeeeezzzeee! I'm sooo glad you are heeeeeere . . . ," Constance called out, her stomach jumping into her throat, as she floated through the air. "Ooooohh ohheeee!" she cried in nervous excitement.

They were flitting here and there like feathers riding a down draft. Before they reached what looked to be the very bottom, Constance suddenly felt herself being sucked toward a gargantuan bulge at the base of "Lady Lyste," the center pole they had been floating around.

She let out a scream as she felt herself rushing toward it fast and faster. Within moments, Constance was a hair's breadth from colliding with the bulge!

"Brace yourself, Constance!" Mr. Keeze shouted. Then he addressed the looming, bulging structure.

"Make way! We are coming in, Madame Yorav!"

But before "Madame Yorav" could respond, Constance felt herself making contact with her. To her surprise, instead of feeling her body burst into a billion little pieces, she felt herself plunge deep into the giant bulge.

"*Hoo hooo*! Constance, you're inside Madame Yorav! I'm right behind you!" Mr. Keeze whooped.

Now, as they both penetrated more deeply, the journey felt rubbery and smelled musty in some way. Constance had a sense of fluid and fiber, as though they were traveling through sinew or vegetation. Whatever they were inside of was definitely alive. She found herself slowing down until at last she was standing next to Mr. Keeze under a gigantic teardrop-shaped pod that hung above them. They were staring up at its round opening as their chests were heaving. After he had recovered sufficiently, Mr. Keeze managed to wheeze out:

"Well, my dear Constance, we are here inside Madame Yorav and about to enter Lady Uveol through this portal," Mr. Keeze said, as he pointed up to the round hole above them.

"You will remember that you and your family were inside Sir Raneth and have seen his Microspangoria production facilities in which our Llopen friends are created. Well now, we are here underneath lovely Lady Uveol and we will explore her inner chamber . . . where things are *begun*. Oh, my gars and starters, no . . . my *stars and garters* . . . how thrilling this will be! I am still not getting the names right in your language, but not to worry, all will come round in the end. The point, my dear Miss Amazeling, is that here inside a magnificent Megaspangorium we will witness a *glorious beginning* and with it, the *fulfilling* of Lady Uveol! My favorite part of the job, this is! I delight so in witnessing The Romance of *Xartief.*"

Now that she could see Mr. Keeze again (which was quite comforting), Constance noticed he was puffing out his chest with pride and wiggling his mustache with no small amount of satisfaction over the prospect of showing her what was coming next.

"Lady Uveol, may we come through your portal and enter your inner chamber?" Constance thought Lady Uveol graciously agreed to his request, but she wasn't quite sure how she knew this. It was just a sense she had, but, come to think of it, ever since she had arrived in *Wonder*, Constance could perceive things about everyone or everything they encountered. That was just normal here.

Now, Constance and Mr. Keeze rose up and through the portal above them and into the inner Mega-whatsis Place and came to rest upon a surface that felt soft and kind of bouncy. The egg-shaped chamber was dim, but there was a glow all around them. Constance sensed that this was a glow of expectancy, as if something truly splendid was about to take place.

Music began to fill her ears. It commenced with an almost inaudible whisper of voices layered, one upon another

"Sporocytesporocytesporsyte . . ." sang one voice.

"Meiosismeiosismeiosismeiosismeisis . . ." sang another.

It sounded like she and Mr. Keeize were in the middle of a forest breeze, hearing the flutter of the leaves.

A lilting melody arose above that and was thereafter accompanied by harmonies and rhythms, which increased in volume until the chamber was awash in sound. If the music of the Microspangoria tubes from which the Llopens emerged was earthy, rhythmic, and tribal, this music inside the Megaspangorium chamber was refined, stately, and graceful. It caused Constance to sway lithely, back and forth, and then to dip up and down, from time to time, into a little curtsy.

What did this remind her of? She let the sound of this mystical music roll around inside her head until it retrieved the memory of a familiar song from home. Ah, yes, that was it! This music reminded her very much of the courtly Baroque dance piece Faye had played repeatedly for Constance while she read her history books of the same period.

What did Mom call that dance? A *passacaglia*? Yes, that was it. What a weird name! So, words in her world could be just as weird as those in *Wonder*, Constance concluded. At any rate, that was what the music in the chamber sounded like to her: a courtly Baroque dance. And indeed, what unfolded before Constance and Mr. Keeze was elaborate, elegant choreography.

"The dance of the Cluine," Mr. Keeze whispered reverently as he waved his hand up with a flourish. Just so, the movement began with a single glowing, floating sphere. The sphere appeared above them on the opposite side of a translucent membrane within a womblike sac. They were peering through a window at a very privileged sight. The sphere seemed to gracefully curtsy and then divide in half, becoming her own dance partner!

Together, the two spheres moved elegantly about one another, bowing and then dividing to become four "Cluine," as Mr. Keeze called them. As the visitors watched the display, three of these orbs faded and then disappeared from view, leaving a soloist swaying before them.

It was this remaining ball that began to grow and enlarge. It floated inside the membrane sac that now filled Lady Uveol's entire Megaspangorium chamber. Inside the sac, the soloist divided again and again until Constance could see eight glowing Cluine dancing together. They moved in sync, with one another. Two of the Cluine orbs came from opposite ends of the sac and joined as one, floating into the middle. Three other of these orbs rose and hovered at the top of the sac, and one very special rosy-colored sphere settled gracefully at the bottom of the chamber inside the sac, attended to by two sister orbs.

So it was that the Cluine finished their dance and positioned themselves for the final bow. Each of them had morphed and matured as if they were changing their garments to prepare for an opulent coming-out party. It was a truly captivating sight, for there could not have been any more courtly a dance than was this one.

Everything about it made Constance feel a sense of vital purpose, beauty, and order in all she surveyed.

When the dance ended, the special rosy Cluine positioned at the bottom center drew Constance's undivided attention. She felt at once that this particular orb bore the countenance of a shy and blushing bride. The Bride took her place as the music ended, accompanied by her two orb sisters. It was then that Mr. Keeze pointed to the final arrangement of the lights and marveled.

"Ah, the Cluine have completed their dance of transformation. Now Lady Uveol has been prepared!"

As Constance looked on, it seemed like everything around her radiated with anticipation and possibility. Lady Uveol's womblike sac had indeed been prepared for something, enlivened by the exquisite dance of the beauteous Bride and her Cluine sisters. How strange and how lovely an occurrence this was!

Constance and Mr. Keeze continued to peer through the translucent membrane of the sac before them and they could see that The Bride was positively incandescent, having turned a deep hue of pink. She curtsied modestly, as did her attendants.

"Xartief be extolled!" she exuded.

"Xartief be extolled, indeed!" Mr. Keeze echoed.

In fact, all around them, Lady Uveol's chamber quivered reverentially at the sound of the word, "Xartief."

"There it is again!" Constance puzzled. "What is it about that word?"

Before she could ponder the thought, Mr. Keeze declared, "Now we await The Negreation, oh no . . . that's not it . . . we await *The Generation* — that's it, *The Generation!*"

At the mention of this, The Bride orb seemed to blush all the more as her attendants modestly retreated. At this moment, when Constance could hardly contain her curiosity about what would happen next, Mr. Keeze plopped himself down upon the floor of Lady Uveol's inner chamber, and in mere moments, proceeded to . . . doze off!

"Oh brother! What in the world is he doing? This place can be so contchumate-ing . . . no! It's *consternating*! Just so frustrating!" Constance muttered to herself.

But before she started to come unglued, she deposited herself beside Mr. Keeze with resignation and proceeded to fall, almost immediately, into a sound sleep. There Constance sat, leaning upon her companion, breathing heavily and dreaming of dancing spheres of light, as a haunting voice whispered:

"Xartief be extolled! Xartief be extolled! Xartief be extolled . . ." over and over and over.

CHAPTER 13

Soaring, Sliding, Splashing, and Surprising!

WHIZZING, WHIRRING, AND RISING RAPIDLY INTO THE atmosphere, Frank, Faye, Charleston, Chance, and Chief flew away on the Llopinator, which had left Mr. Keeze and Constance behind, drowning out Constance's cries in the deafening whir of the propellers or whatever they were. The ascending Faultsoms flew into the enormity of a sky so magnificent that they felt it drench their souls in a kind of revelation.

From time to time, Mistress Bublem Eeb would descend and land upon continents of glorious color, and the Faultsoms would hear her slurp and hum to herself contentedly before she launched again into the cerulean expanse of sky. If Frank and Faye hadn't been so concerned about Constance, they would have enjoyed the ride immensely, but their hearts were troubled with an anxiety that only parents can truly know, even in *Wonder*.

The boys, on the other hand, were entirely exhilarated and, frankly, not unhappy at all to have Constance, with her often bossy big-sisterness, far away. To Charleston, Chance, and Chief this was the best ride of their young lives. It couldn't have been any better if they were taking a rocketship stocked with gummy worms and french fries all the way to the moon!

And so, the fantastic journey continued with stops in between to dispatch Llopen passengers at various destinations and, apparently, to refuel. Somehow Frank, Faye, and the boys stayed aloft and board together, taking in the exhilarating journey.

Suddenly, a massive gust of wind blew Mistress Eeb backward for quite a distance, and then upside down and around in circles. The Faultsoms experienced G-Forces that made their heads spin and their insides almost turn into outsides.

"Aaaahhhhh!"

"Eeeeeeeeeekkk!"

"He—lllllppppp!"

They screamed their heads off in sheer terror. All except for Chance, who couldn't get enough of this wild ride; his screams were shrieks of sheer delight. The Llopens, as well, were having a marvelous time, continuing their high-octane chatter with inexhaustible excitement. Chance shared in their wild, exuberant outbursts, fitting right in with them.

"Oooooahhhh! What a riiiiiiiddde! De—liiiiightful!" the Llopens yelled.

"Oh yeeeeaaah, way cooooooollll! Dudes, check this out, we are doing 360s!" Chance hollered. As was his way in almost any new setting, he had instantly made friends of the Llopens and together they revelled in the thrills of the flight together.

After several circles and upside-down to rightside-up maneuvers, the Llopinator managed to steady herself and fly straight into the wind with intense resolve. Eventually, the gusts began to weaken, and their flight pattern leveled off. Seemingly in need of a rest, however, Mistress Eeb landed upon a vivid pink landscape and everything fell silent. There the Llopinator sat, apparently in utter exhaustion, with her body heaving as if to catch her breath.

As they sat quietly upon the pink tarmac, the family thought about what this flying thing was and how they knew "she" was breathing? How was it that everything in *Wonder* seemed to be singing and communicating thoughts and feelings to them? The longer they were in this strange realm, the more the Faultsoms became attuned to the language of *Wonder*.

As they collected themselves, Chance managed to sprawl out on his Llopen sofa, energy expended, enjoying the high of his spinning head. Charleston, on the other hand, sat erect, quietly calming himself, breathing deeply and listening to the amazing storm of music that echoed in his ears.

"Hey, Hon . . . Hon? Ah, you okay over there?" Frank called hesitantly to Faye, who had nearly passed out and was babbling incoherently to herself:

"Get . . . the clothes, get the clothes out of the dryer. I can't make it stop . . . somebody . . . please turn off the dryer — now!" Faye's brain was on tumble dry, and Frank was a bit "green around the gills" himself.

A whimpering sound came from Chief atop his Llopen:

"Cheeperths, Ma . . . I think I'm gonna be thick . . . Maaaaaah?!"
He was curled up in a ball, considering whether or not he would
puke, but ultimately decided against it.

This break in the action was most welcome to all of them, but
in *Wonder*, if nothing happens, it is not for very long. Just as soon
they each started to find the bottom of their stomachs again and
their inner gyroscopes had reoriented, the Llopens, upon which the
Faultsoms were deposited, began to disembark from Mistress Eeb,
barking orders to one another.

"Move 'em out, fellows!"

" It's our turn to be deployed!"

"Time to be off!"

With that, the family found themselves upon some sort of sticky,
limey green landing pad and were released from the goo that was
keeping them attached to the Llopens ever since they had left the
Microspangoria tubes inside of "Sir Raneth." Now they were able to
walk about freely on the fibrous surface of the tarmac.

A moment later, Mistress Eeb, apparently having recovered from
her exhaustion, took off, leaving the family surrounded by cheering
Llopens shouting their goodbyes and appreciation for the "lift."

"Goodbye!"

"Thank you for the journeying, Mistress Eeb!"

"Ho Ho, toodle-oo!"

Then they returned to their mission.

"Here were are at last, fellows! Well worth the wait! It's time to
Down and Dig, Down and Dig!"

"Goodbye, Mistress!"

"Yes, yes, yes, Down and Dig. Let's get to it, boys!"

At this, the Llopens began to chant a silly refrain that Chance
and Chief found quite amusing. It was the kind of song that only
goofy adolescent boys seem to appreciate, but Charleston, ever the
serious one, couldn't help but find it catchy as well.

> Downnitty down, down da down!
> Diggitty dig, dig da dig!
> Downnitty down da diggity dig!
> Da down a diggitty down-a-down dig!
> Stigmastyle, a stigmastyle.
> We'll be Down Downing a Stigmastyle

"Again, lads, let's sing it again!" a Llopen shouted. And so they all began again, but this time they belted it out as a round, with Llopens entering, over and over again, at different times. It seemed to go on forever until Faye and Frank thought their skulls would explode, while the boys, much to their parents' chagrin, added to the cacophony by chanting along at the top of their lungs.

"Frank?? Frank . . . make it stop. I thought the clothes were out of the dryer . . . but it sounds like it's still running . . . make it stop! Frank?"

Faye was still trying to sort herself out after their frenzied flight as Frank made his way over to her and wrapped his Llopen-sticky arms around her shoulders and held her close. He gently kissed her tacky forehead and whispered into her ear:

"It's okay sweetie, it's gonna be okay . . ."

The family stood on the spongy landing pad surrounded by the ever-nattering Llopens, when the sky abruptly darkened and immense plops of water hit the landing pad around them. If this was rain, the drops were the size of boulders, more like water bombs than drops. Much to their dismay, Frank and Faye were hit by an enormous plop of water, nearly flattening them. They were instantly soaked and utterly shocked!

"Eieieieehhh! Aaahhhhhh!" came their shrieks of surprise and outrage.

It would be an understatement to say that they were not at all happy about this development, but their boys, on the other hand, thought it was hilarious!

Charleston, Chance, and Chief stood, their hands over their mouths, and snorted as they tried to contain their snickering. All of a sudden, several more massive water bombs came out of the sky and landed right atop the boys, dousing them thoroughly and knocking them down — which now Frank and Faye found quite amusing. What a ludicrous, soggy shambles they all were, but this was nothing compared to the sight of the Llopens!

Their chattering was swiftly squelched by water plops falling upon them as well. The outlandish orange fuzz balls now looked utterly ridiculous and forlorn, with their wet droopy fur straggling down. They were quite the dazed, deflated lot of fellows, and the Faultsoms, one and all, burst into great peals of laughter at the sight of them. It was a deep and refreshing laugh they shared together. And once the Llopens had recovered from their own shock and surprise, they joined them in the merriment.

As it happened, the rain bombs had washed the Llopen goo off the Faultsoms completely. They stood in the afterglow of these comic events, noticing that the skies above them had cleared and a luscious cinnamon-roll kind of warmth was pouring down upon them, quickly drying them up.

At the same time, the soggy Llopens all about them began to swell. It seemed like they might burst open, but then, from inside each one, a snakelike appendage emerged. Each of these wiggling Llopen arms worked its way out and toward the center of the limey landing pad, found an opening, and pushed itself down inside of it.

One Llopen shouted his greetings to the landing surface they all stood upon, as his snakey outgrowth emerged and dug into it.

"Salutations to you, Miss Mistag! You are a marvy place to light upon! We are coming in . . . the Down and Dig does now begin!"

"Downitty down down da down! What fun!" A Llopen right next to the Faultsoms began to chant.

"Hey there, Lad Amazeling!" he cried out to Chance,

"You seem a jolly sort. Why not join me for The Downing! I shall make a way in for you."

Needing no more encouragement, Chance ran to the snakelike arm thing, dove toward it headfirst, and vanished!

"Oh, Crime-in-itly! Is there no way to keep track of anyone here?!" Frank blurted out in frustration and alarm.

"Come on, guys!" he shouted.

And wasting no time, he took Faye by the hand, ran forward, and jumped toward the Llopen appendage just as Chance had. They both disappeared, followed quickly by Chief and Charleston.

Each had made quite a leap of faith into what turned out to be a tube, and their arrival was a slippery one, for they did not land on a floor but found themselves sliding down the inside of the tube as the "Downing Song" echoed around them.

They were slipping on some kind of fluid and just ahead, they could see two gleaming blue orbs sliding in front of them and a glowing red one lighting the way. The tube was a tunnel, no, a slide. No, it was a living, growing tunnel slide! They could see the end of it just past the orbs ahead, but each time they thought they would all hit a wall or crash through one and fall into utter oblivion, the tubeslide grew longer right before them!

Chief loved slides and this one was the ultimate of slides. As the Faultsoms slid down farther and farther, it occurred to Chie that it might never end! It could go on and on as the tunnel kept growing and growing and might never have to stop. This was another adventure tailor-made for the Faultsom boys.

As he slid down, Chance's brain was filled with ideas and applications for a self-elongating transport device that he could create if he ever got back home. Charleston felt that he was discovering new depths of knowing and of understanding *the way of love*, as he watched the two blue spheres and their red lantern guide his family to the brink of a continuing precipice upon a living conduit that never let them collide or fall.

And what about Frank and Faye? Somehow the thorough washing they'd received from the rain bombs not only refreshed them but also imparted a new vigor, just as the light shower had done when they first arrived in *Wonder* and were all so full of defeat and dread. Showers here were a cleansing, revitalizing flow that didn't just clean their bodies but also lifted their spirits, even as *Wonder*'s warmth didn't only dry them but embraced their souls with reassurance.

As a result, and much to their boys' amazement, Frank and Faye were having a ball remembering their favorite childhood sliding experiences. Here they were slipping along inside of this incredible living tunnel with a giddiness that overtook all their adult inhibitions and their anxieties about Constance. They were whooshing through memories of sliding into big splashy puddles with their galoshes on, and the final slides of the day that helped them overcome sad goodbyes. They remembered the train rides down slippery surfaces with favored playmates, familiar friendly slides they mastered easily, and big daunting slides that demanded their bravery but rewarded them with feelings of invincibility. They remembered all these, and they recalled the happy faces waiting for them at the bottom of their best slidings and they could feel again the safety of their parents' arms that had scooped them up just as their feet touched the ground.

Frank and Faye relived these experiences as they watched the glowing orbs ahead plunging them into the darkness of a tunnel that extended right in front of their eyes, all the way down. As if this wasn't astonishing enough, they realized that the angle of their descent inside the living tunnel was almost straight down! It was a scary, thrilling feeling and yet they felt supported somehow. This was a miracle for the easily queasy Faye.

As they continued to slide, Faye and Frank and the boys began to discern the temperaments of the two blue spheres that led their way. The Llopens had been immature and goofy and could be quite annoying, but these new entities were of a much more sober demeanor. The one that ventured forth first, behind the red lantern orb, was a bright blue color and it morphed into a royal, iridescent purple the farther they descended. The sphere seemed to grow in nobility and change color as the journey continued. There was a knightly quality to him, and the Faultsoms knew that he was on a mission.

The other orb that followed behind was also blue but developed a luminous turquoise cast along the way. They were like a knight and squire riding forth on a quest with the lantern of the red sphere leading before them. And it was as if the tubeslide was a horse with boundless stamina upon which they rode toward the object of their zeal.

How long the descent took, none of them could say, but the Faultsoms would later recount that for The Knight and Squire, the journey had the quality of a quest, as if it were a voyage of preparation and transformation. The two morphing blue orbs were of a single purpose, but each with a different role to play.

The Faultsoms continued their slide deeper and deeper down, and after what seemed like ages, they finally reached the bottom, where the family could hear the next verse of the Llopen song.

"Diggitty dig, dig da dig . . ." the song went on as the tunnel leveled off and moved forward more or less horizontally.

They craned their necks to look past one another and watched as the end of the tubeslide tipped upward. It ascended and they could see its now open end pass through a hole in a thick wall. Then it dug upward and into what seemed to be a very large chamber. When the tube had penetrated the enclosure, the red lantern orb receded, as The Knight and Squire gathered themselves, preparing to make a dignified entrance into it. It was as though they squared their shoulders, which of course orbs cannot do. But the Faultsoms could see that the Knight, now a golden-flecked purple, and The Squire, now a vivid turquoise, each possessed a confident and noble bearing as they sallied forth out of the tunnel. At this, the silly "Diggity Dig Digging" refrain transformed into the music of a Grand Purpose reverberating all around them and the family sensed that something of great importance was about to unfold. Excited to see what it was, they scrambled after The Knight and The Squire climbing up and out of the tubeslide as quickly as they could.

What the Faultsoms saw when they emerged from the tunnel was quite a surprise. There on the floor of an enormous egg-shaped, dimly lit, and womblike chamber sat Mr. Keeze and Constance, leaning upon one another, fast asleep and snoring loudly.

CHAPTER 14

The Generation

"XARTIEF BE EXTOLLED! XARTIEF BE EXTOLLED!" CONSTANCE heard the rosy-pink dancing balls of light whisper to her, again and again, as they swayed to the music of their otherworldy passacaglia. A strange feeling overtook her and she felt herself lift up and out of her body. She floated over a snoring Mr. Keeze and began to take her place among the courtly maidens before her.

She had never felt so pretty, or graceful, or valuable. She was one of the loveliest of the ladies, strong, beautiful, and part of a Grand Purpose. She wasn't striving and she was not trying to be perfect. She wasn't feeling misunderstood or left out, and it wasn't her job to make things happen. She was in perfect sync with her surroundings, playing a unique role in what was utterly essential to the completion of the dance, yet she felt free to express herself in flowing fancies of movement, with no fear of making mistakes and no responsibility for everything around her.

She found herself chanting that strange word with the other dancers:

"Xartief . . . Xartief . . . Xartief be extolled!"

She knew that all of this movement and mystery was The Way of Xartief. She *knew* this . . . even as *she was known*, entirely.

Floating glowingly and gloriously, she thrilled to the dance and her part in it, when the maidens around her began to circle and curtsy to her, and give her an honor far above their own.

"Miss Amazeling, Beauteous Constance, you are Bride, Generation awaits you." This took Constance's breath away.

Could this be true? *She* was The Bride? That gorgeous creature that carried such compelling power and grace?

"Beauteous Constance, you are Bride, and Generation awaits you," they repeated.

"Xartief be extolled!"

The atmosphere around her was quaking with the presence of Xartief . . .

Constance shuddered.

"Hey, wake up, Sleeping Beauty! You were snoring like a water buffalo with a head cold!" Chance was briskly shaking his sister as a relieved Faye and Frank bent down over her and the snoring Mr. Keeze. Chief chimed in. "Hey Thith! Wake up! We've been flying and thliding! Have you been thleeping thith whole time?"

Constance awakened, her eyes widening as she took in her surroundings. The vision of the orbs and their music faded as she blinked and stared up at the sight of her endearingly kooky family.

"Arise and Shine, Constance. I'm so glad you are no worse for the wear, sister." Charleston offered a hand up to his groggy sis as Chance slapped her on the back.

"Hey Con. Just like you to sleep through this whole deal!"

Constance was swarmed by her family pack. "Conthtance!" Chief shouted as he jumped into her arms, gave her a wet smack on the cheek, and mashed her head against his.

Faye and Frank wrapped themselves around her and sighed deeply at the sight of her. How Constance had missed them and their irritating but loveable Faultsom Foolishness!

Mr. Keeze roused himself, awakened by the hubbub.

"Ah, The Amazings — all here together as it should be! My favorite part of the job, this is . . . seeing things come together! Penstudous! No, no, no . . . it's simply *stupendous*! I trust you enjoyed your journey. Mistress Amazeling and I have had quite the time ourselves."

With that came all the exclamations and hugs and stories. It was a Faultsom free-for-all as everyone started to talk at once, stumbling over one another's words and trying to stitch the pieces of their various stories together to make sense of their adventures.

As he watched his family members all fighting to get a word in edgewise, Frank stood back with arms folded, smiling as he shook his head. This was *his* whacky family, all right. Charleston also withdrew from the fray to analyze the happenings.

"Hmmm, the velocity of the wind gusts must have blown us right back to where Constance and Mr. Keeze disembarked the Llopinator."

Frank had heard him and picked up his train of thought.

"What are the odds of that?"

Chance piggy-backed on the idea.

"Yeah, and what are the chances of us digging our way into the same room where Constance was sitting there snoring like a cyclone? Snnnnooock, Sunnnnch!" He went on to imitating her snores in the loudest, most annoying way possible just to watch her raise her left eyebrow in perturbed protest.

"Chodds and Ances!" Mr. Keeze exclaimed. "*Odds and Chances*!? Odds — Chances?? Not in *Wonder*! That's nuff and stonsense . . . no! It's just plain *stuff and nonsense*, that! Nothing around here is a matter of odds and chances" He shook his head in disbelief at the thought.

The family's riotous reunion was in full swing when the already faint light around them in the chamber dimmed even more and the music of *Grand Purpose* swelled about them. A spotlight descended upon the scene and a hush fell upon the Faultsoms as The Knight and Squire advanced past them and through what seemed to be a silky veil.

They entered the sac in which the lovely blushing Bride and her attendant Maidens-in-Waiting were hovering expectantly. The feeling of anticipation was unmistakable. It hung like a warm, thick mist in the air. The courtly dance music of the Cluine now began to intertwine with the music of the Knight and Squire and their quest.

Faye and Frank, Constance, Charleston, Chance, and Chief watched expectantly as The Knight moved boldly into the presence of The Bride and presented himself before her, bowing low. As he approached, she blushed as ample and deep a crimson as that of a living, beating heart swelling with valor and courage, and then she shyly gave a nod to The Knight.

In a flash of ardor that caused the Faultsoms to turn their heads away in reverent modesty, The Knight advanced passionately toward The Bride and the two were engulfed in one another. It was an instant of unspeakable intimacy and transcendent glory. This was the moment of The Generation, for when Knight and Bride moved into one another, something began. Something new became alive that had not been alive before.

There was an explosion of light and color, and the ringing of a new song inside the inner chamber of Lady Uveol as the Bride and Knight and their attendants were playing out this drama. The entire space was throbbing with energy.

What unfolded had flowered in a moment that forever glimmered in each Faultsom. Their souls were somehow reshaped by the sight of what was being created inside this secret place of *Wonder*. As The Generation continued, Knight and Bride were indiscernible from one another. They were fully merged — married together, and a new being resulted.

The Faultsoms turned back to see the little life burst forth, and they looked on in stupefied fascination. Not only was a new being developing but The Lantern, Squire, and Maiden orbs, who had surrounded and supported The Bride and Knight in this great quest had now surrendered themselves to a deeper purpose. They had morphed into what seemed like an embracing circle of sustenance for the little being, which had been generated before their eyes in the inner chamber.

The family stood together, speechless (which was no small thing for the Faultsoms), until Faye broke the silence in typical family fashion.

"Does anyone have a tissue?" she snivelled.

Tears were streaming down her face and goop was dripping from her nose and from the noses of all the sniffling Faultsoms around her. Frank and the boys were not waiting for tissues. They dragged their sleeves across their runny noses until their arms were covered in snot. Constance was weeping as she threw herself on her daddy's chest, shoulders heaving, and she cried:

"The Bride, Daddy, The Bride! He came to her and they made a new life. It is so . . . beautiful and it's . . . true . . . it's so *true!*"

Faye came from behind them to wrap an arm around her boys, pulling them together in a rowdy jumble as she frantically fished into the pocket of her colorful gypsy-styled pantaloons. Somehow, there inside a floppy pocket she found a balled up wad of tissues, one for each Faultsom to blow in to. This was a little marvel for which she was exceedingly grateful as, only a mother can be.

Drenching their tissues, the family stood together, crying and wiping, and loudly tooting their noses like trumpets until they began to laugh. They laughed and laughed until they couldn't contain their joy. At the height of their laughter they heard loud sobbing next to them and turned to see Mr. Keeze, whom they had forgotten in all the excitement.

"Oh my . . . my, my, my my. My favorite part of the job, this is . . . it's so yovell!" He was so moved he didn't even try to correct himself. (Dear reader, perhaps you will find that you can unravel his *Wonder* word.)

His face was red and tears dripped down his enormous mustache, soaking the stripes on his fancy Gate Keeper's uniform. Pulling out an oversized ruffled white handkerchief (the size of a table cloth), he blew his nose with a hornlike blast that shook the chamber.

"This just undoes me every time." He blew again. "What romance! What mystery! What magnificence! A Generation! A beginning!" Mr. Keeze blew another blast.

"The Knight and Brave, Beautiful Bride have married and produced a new life, which will fulfill Lady Uveol! Xartief be extolled!" At this the Faultsoms found themselves cheering out loud:

"Xartief be extolled!"

But they had no more than a few moments to bask in the glory of The Generation, for the new little being and its surrounding nourishment were growing fast and filling up the inner chamber, squeezing the Faultsom family against its walls. They were in the growing belly of Lady Uveol as she was being fulfilled by the new life, and the family needed out!

"Mama, it's getting squithy in here!" Chief cried.

"I'm hot!" Chance said as he began to drip perspiration.

Faye was alarmed. "I don't think we will fit in here for very long. In fact, there really isn't any room left! Frank?!?"

Frank had already assessed the situation and was pushing against the chamber walls, trying to make space for his family, but it was of no use.

"Mr. Keeze! Help!" He shouted in panic. But Mr. Keeze, still preoccupied with what they had all just witnessed, was oblivious to their dire circumstance.

Now, their faces were smashed up again the chamber wall as the sac before them grew to fill up every inch of space. But Mr. Keeze was quite unresponsive. He just stood next to them, transfixed by what he had witnessed as the life continued to grow before him.

"What do we do now, Mr. Keeze?" Charleston choked out his words.

"Mom, I can't breathe! I'm suffocating!" Constance wailed. "Dad, do something!"

"Mr. Keeze??" They all screamed.

The Faultsoms were trapped and running out of time.

CHAPTER 15

ꟾExpansion, ꟾExpulsion, and ꟾExile

JUST WHEN THEY THOUGHT THEY WERE GOING TO SUFFO-
cate, the Faultsoms heard a compressed voice cry out.

"Amazings, follow me!" Mr. Keeze suddenly took command.
"Quickly, there! Get down on your hands and knees! There is still a
way out."

They managed to pull their bodies down to the floor, sliding
themselves along the spongy chamber wall against which they were
being squished. There they found just enough room to crawl toward
the opening which was in the center of the chamber. This was the
hole that had been their doorway inside. Headfirst and one by one,
they dropped out of Lady Uveol's belly, tumbling down onto the surface below. And just in time, too, for the Lady's belly was now completely full and expanding outward and downward above them while
the portal they had come through sealed itself up tightly, just as the
last Faultsom escaped and hit the floor.

They sat for a moment gazing upward and noticed that Lady Uveol's exterior was changing. Her skin, originally of a rather rubbery quality, was now hardening and darkening. Somehow the family knew that it was becoming a protective layer to ensure the safety of the new little one still inside her. And this layer, they knew, was like a dark brown coat she was donning in preparation for a journey.

Just then, Madame Yorav began to vibrate, causing everything to shudder and shake. (Dear Reader, you will remember this: Madame Yorav is the structure around Lady Uveol, who Constance feared she was going to crash into.)

Scccrreeeecchhhh! Zzzcchhhhheeeekkkkksh!!

A rubbery, stretching, ear-piercing sound rent the atmosphere. It was much like the sound the Faultsoms had heard when they were inside Sir Raneth in the midst of the Llopen population explosion, just before the ceiling above them burst open. This time, however, the squeaking was coming from all around them. It was intensifying rapidly and the family tried to bury their heads and cover their ears to shield themselves from its piercing power.

"Madame Yorav is about to blow! Hatten down the Batches!? *Batten down the hatches*!!" they heard Mr. Keeze shout out.

Clutching desperately to one another, they shut their eyes tightly and braced themselves. They were being shaken to the core and it felt like their brains were turning into mush and their eardrums were about to implode.

At the peak of the awful sounds and shudders, the Faultsom family, along with Mr. Keeze, were tossed upward and violently expelled out of Madame Yorav, who had burst open on all sides! As they flew through the air, they caught sight of Lady Uveol dressed in her dark brown coat, flying through the air along with what seemed to be many other ladies uveol who, as it turned out, had also been inside of Madame Yorav!

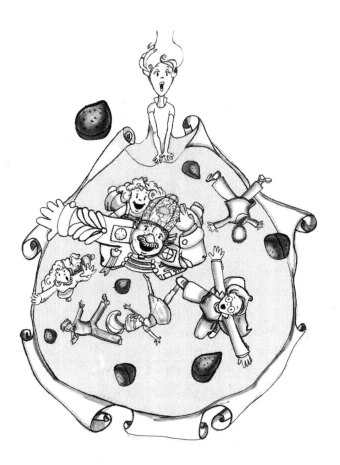

In a split second, the family experienced a thousand sensations. Sailing through midair, their minds raced to process what was happening. Mr. Keeze flew past them, giggling wildly and screaming,

"Fa———vo———rite parrrrrtttt of the jo——bbb . . . thissss isssss!"

Now, for the second time during their adventure in *Wonder*, the family burst out from an enclosed space that had erupted due to an explosion of expanding energy. For a second time, they were engulfed in an expanse of pure blue, which utterly awed them. This time, however, they were accompanied by scads of ladies, all in their brown coats, who had also been sprayed into the wind.

As Frank and Faye and the kids rocketed through the sky, something very peculiar began to happen. They felt like they were moving through molasses and, in slow motion, there was a bizarre reshaping of their perspectives taking place. Not only was time dilating; their bodies were dilating as well. They were expanding in size, and as they grew, the scope of the landscape below was changing.

For the first time since being in *Wonder*, they could not only see sky, above them but could also discern a horizon line. The land they were hurtling over had originally looked like an infinite blur of color. Now the various hues were becoming distinct and separate. Next, they could see in greater detail the shapes below them, and noticed that these were configured in groups of colors, each with different attributes. They felt that if they got close enough, they could actually reach out and scoop up the colorful clumps with their hands.

Hands?!! Their hands now revealed the scale of their bodies against the backdrop of the landscape below them. Now, as they stretched out their extremities, they realized their bodies were actually larger than the bunches of color that had once seemed to them to be the size of entire continents! Not only that, but the dark-coated ladies who had loomed large over the Faultsoms when they were all expelled from Madame Yorav had diminished so much they were now teensy little specks that could almost disappear in the palms of their hands. These little flecks flew past them, spreading out and falling upon patches of bare ground that appeared here and there below them.

The ground! Another marvel! They could now see the ground and could tell that the batches of color below them were beds and bushes of flowers.

"Ah, Amazings . . . here we are!" Mr. Keeze announced as the expansion of their bodies was completed and their motion slowed to a stop.

He hovered briefly and then landed with a merry little bounce upon the ground. Bustling about, he put himself in order, because he had arrived quite rumpled by the ejection and expansion during the flight. With amusingly officious flare, he cinched up his wide shiny black belt with its impressive gold buckle, straightened his epaulets, fluffed the oversized handkerchief he had hastily stuffed back into his pocket, petted his mustache, and tipped his key-covered helmet very precisely, so that it sat at a jaunty angle upon his head.

The Faultsoms now hovered in the air for a few moments before landing gracefully in an extraordinary field of flowers which extended beyond the horizon on either side of them: crimsons, purples, yellows, and oranges complimented with dashes of brilliant blues and greens vibrated in the sunlight emitting the same delicious fragrance that had filled their senses just before Mistress Bublem Eeb had landed above them after Sir Raneth's ceiling had burst open.

"I remember that fragrance . . . it's . . . it's heavenly!" cried Faye.

The Faultsoms, one and all, breathed in the sumptuous scent and felt their heads spinning even as their spirits rose in waves of joy.

"Everybody, look closely at these flowers around us . . . I can't explain it but things are starting to make sense to me . . . ," said Frank as the family crowded around him, bending over a nearby flower to closely examine it.

Everything they saw in the blossom seemed oddly familiar to them even though from this perspective it didn't look like anything they remembered knowing much about before. Still, they did know the flower, *intimately*, from the *inside out*. The Faultsoms were lost in this thought and enjoying the lovely fragrance, when Chief squealed with delight:

"Hey! Look! I think thith ith Mithtreth Eeb!"

Lo and behold, a tubby-looking bumble bee with a winsome and industrious air landed on Chief's nose and seemed to buzz out a greeting to him before loopily flitting off to slurp up more of the honeyed nectar she was imbibing at each stop. Everywhere they looked, they could see birds and butterflies flitting back and forth, each finding their favorite blossoms to rest upon. Attracted by the enchanting candy colors and enticing intoxicants, the pollinators leisurely flew in and out, pleasuring themselves with the luscious floral elixirs.

As the various creatures whizzed by them the Faultsoms thought they could hear wee voices. No, it couldn't be! But . . . it was true! The family could just make out the faint but inevitably boisterous chorus of chattering voices.

"Hey Ho, fellows, we are off . . . !"

"Up and away . . . awaaaayyy!" They recognized the familiar, friendly fracas.

"Ith the Llopenth!" "Yay! The Llopens!" Chief and Chance each exclaimed. The little wise guys were in their usual frenzy riding along on the Llopinators. As they whizzed past Charleston, he suddenly let loose a violent fit of sneezing.

"AhhhhhChooooo! Oh Doh!" He cried as his sinuses clogged up. "I'm allergic to the Llopens — why, doh!" Charleston's brilliant brain was at work. "They are dot Llopeds, they are *polleds — polled graids,*" he cried stuffily. "I am allergic to theb!"

Now, Constance joined into the sneezing fest, her eyes watering and her nose clogging.

"We were tidy and we were stuck on those whacky polled guys. We bust have been bicroscopic! It's a miracle we did'dit explode from our allergies!" She spoke with a stuffy-headed sound just before her latest sneeze erupted. "Achoooooohhh!"

"Yeah!" interjected Chance. "We were just specks stuck on those *pollen grains* that were riding on Mistress Bublem Eeb . . . "

"Why, yes . . . Mistress *Bumble Bee!*" Faye cried.

Frank continued:

"And we were there when the Llopens — the *pollens* — grew out of what Mr. Keeze called the 'Microspangoria' inside Sir Raneth! Hmmm . . ." Frank was starting to decode these weird words, in his head.

"We were thtuck to the pollens' yellow futh!" shouted Chief.

"Charlie, it is quite astonishing that we didn't sneeze ourselves id to a coba!" Constance shouted with stuffiness.

"It's like someone decreased the effects of the allergens so we could survive . . . remarkable . . ." Charleston mused as he tried to muffle a building sneeze.

Then, right on cue for a second time, a welcome phenomenon occurred. Amidst the hubbub of their shared revelations, Charleston's and Constance's allergic reactions miraculously calmed, as a cleansing breeze drifted by them. A welcome *Wonder!*

Frank shushed his jabbering family, motioning them to be still and listen. They could hear the yakking fuzzballs as they sailed away.

"Goodbye, Amazings! We are off to Down and Dig! Down and Dig!" cried the hyperactive histamine instigators.

"Goodbye, Llopens! Goodbye!" The Faultsoms shouted back incredulously.

Pollen?? They were talking to pollen grains!

As if their previous *Wonderful* experiences hadn't been whacky enough, the Faultsoms were now even more astonished, as they took in the dazzling sights and fragrances of the infinitely varied flowers in the endless fields that stretched about them. They marveled at all of this as they revelled in their bizarre memories.

Frank scratched his head as flashes from his university plant-biology classes continued to invade his mind.

"Hmmmm . . . well this *is* really something!" he said as he retrieved everyone's focus with excited gesticulations. "Kids, it looks like we have just been on an incredible — no, a simply *Wonderous* journey! We've just delved into the secret life of a flower!" Frank was pondering the various plant parts and processes they had experienced.

"Why yes, Father! I suspect, we've witnessed flower propagation," Charleston added, recalling a botany book that he'd absorbed not too long ago.

"Oh my . . . *imagine* that!" Faye marveled.

"Papa, wath propa—pro-pa-gathan?" Chief asked.

Bending down to look into his youngest boy's eyes and pull him in for a big bear hug, Frank, answered:

"Why, Chiefy, that's the way flowers reproduce — the way they make new little baby flowers."

Now, the pieces began to fall rapidly into place, and what the family did not yet fully understand about the microscopic world of flower biology, nevertheless became real to them. This experiential knowledge ignited an insatiable, lifelong curiosity about gardens and flowers, which had quite a mysterious impact in their lives.

It was at this point that Mr. Keeze stepped forward into the middle of the bubbling family pack. Clearing his throat and posing as if to make a formal declaration:

"My dear friends, it has been such a delight to usher you around this part of *Wonder*. I shall be sad to see you go. I trust you enjoyed your journey, but the time has come for you to return . . ."

At this pronouncement, a dark shadow fell across their hearts as surely as if a cloud had blotted out the sun. An icy hush chilled the air for quite some time, until at last, Faye's trembling voice cut through the anxious atmosphere that had overtaken them.

"Go . . . back . . ? Go back, Mr. Keeze?" She cried. "We can't go back. If we go back, they will take our kids! They want to teach them that none of this is real!" Faye began to cry as Frank came alongside her and pulled her close.

"It's true, sir, if we go back we will lose our children and they will lose . . . *Wonder*." Frank pleaded for help.

"Hmmmmm . . ." Mr. Keeze considered this, letting out a little whistle. "Yes, I see . . . this *is* a midelma. No, it's quite a serious *dilemma* . . . for there is no avoiding your return."

Their hearts sank, and the kids began to protest while Mr. Keeze scanned their faces. He looked into their eyes with a most somber expression, which stoked their worst fears. Then, looking off into the distance, he wistfully mumbled what sounded like a question into the air. Cocking his head to one side as if listening to someone speak, he intoned:

"Ah, hmmmmm, I see . . . well, then . . ."

Looking back at them with an endearing tenderness, he said, "It must be so, friends, you must go back."

Crestfallen cries and sighs came from the Faultsoms as they realized that their exile was imminent. Mr. Keeze raised his hands and patted the air as if to calm them.

"Now, now. Have you learned nothing here, my friends? Look closely at what is happening around you. Do you not see, do you not yet understand what is right under your noses?"

He waved his hand and bowed with a flourish, as he always did when he was excited and proud to reveal something they had not seen before. As they followed the sweep of his hand, their eyes again beheld vast fields of flowers and happy birds, butterflies, and bees flitting here and there.

"What you need to know right now is here in front of you." He pointed to the flowers around them, nodding his head. "Go and *see* . . . my friends. *Go . . . and . . . see!*"

CHAPTER 16

Seeing and Supposing

IT WAS A SOBER AND RESTRAINED BUNCH OF FAULTSOMS who considered their fate as *Wonder's* gentle wind curled around their shoulders that afternoon, bringing with it whispers of comfort. They were facing a crisis that would forever change their family, and Mr. Keeze had asked them to go and look at . . . *plants*? As if that would make any difference in such a dire situation! Well, at least, they thought, the continuing plant-biology lesson would delay their inevitable return.

And so, with bowed heads and heavy hearts, the Faultsoms wandered off, each mysteriously drawn to the little coated ladies who were here and there floating on the breeze and showering down upon the earth. As one child headed off to the left, one went to the right. Another stopped a stone's throw away, and the last one rambled almost out of view, mother and father watching as their slump-shouldered kids meandered in the field, each one following a floating seed.

Why of course! That's what they were. The family members began to realize that the little coated ladies were actually *seeds*! This realization dawned upon them one by one, as fascination overcame sadness and the Faultsoms picked up their pace, each chasing after a particular seed to see where it would land. Then they knelt, bent, or sat down, digging their fingers into *Wonder*'s topsoil, waiting to see what would happen next.

As soon as the seeds made contact with the dirt, a wisp of *Wonderwind* mysteriously whipped up around them, creating perfect little tornados of dirt and dust encircling the seeds and burying them under rich, dark loam. And once the seeds were hidden from view, a marvelous thing happened: Frank and Faye, Constance, Charleston, Chance, and Chief were given the ability to see *into* the ground! Not only that, but the process of seed germination played out before them at an outlandish speed, like accelerated time-lapse photography!

They each watched a tiny seed burrow snugly into the earth as moisture and warmth penetrated its stout little protective jacket. Then they saw a world *within* a world. They were able to look not only into the ground but under the coat and *inside the seed itself*! They hadn't seen a seed that close-up since they were inside Lady Uveol, peering into her womblike chamber where they had witnessed The Generation when The Knight and Bride cells had merged.

Now, Frank had a major revelation: Lady Uveol was an *Ovule*.

"Why, this is another one of Mr. Keeze's mixed-up words!" Frank exclaimed. "Uveol! Of course! The word is actually *ovule*! And . . . that would mean that Madame "Yorav" is actually the *ovary* of the flower. Of course! And an ovule is produced inside the ovary!"

Then Frank recalled that *ovule* was another word for *egg* — and when a flower's egg is fertilized, it becomes a *seed*! This is what they had watched when The Knight cell merged with The Bride cell in The Generation! The family had also witnessed the transformation of the other plant cells into the nourishment a new life would need. Why, they had observed The Knight and Squire *sperm* cells uniting with the *nuclei*! Funny Mr. Keeze had called the *nuclei* "The Cluine."

Now, the Faultsoms could all see that The Generation had actually produced a *tiny baby plant* that was hidden inside each seed coat, complete with its teensy leaf shoots, root, stem, and stored food. Indefatigably, each of these little embryos, now buried in *Wonder's* earth, pushed its roots out of its shell. These persistent little seed sprouters had supersized strength!

The root sprouts wiggled downward, deeper into the soil, and then thrust their leaf-sprout tendrils upward and out of the ground! The stored food fed and nourished the little plants until they could receive nutrients from sun and soil. Then the Faultsoms looked on in astonishment as, in a flash, the embryos grew into toddler plants, which shot up eagerly toward the warmth of the sunlight. Faye, Frank, Constance, Charleston, Chance, and Chief gawked as the miracle of each plant's growth and maturation unfolded before them in mere moments.

Now, having risen up above the dirt some distance, the maturing plant stems were producing flower buds! The kids shrieked with delight as, one by one, blossoms burst out in radiant blares of color, like kernels of popcorn erupting in a pot of hot oil. Squeals of glee could be heard across the fields, and the Faultsoms were sure they'd heard the mature flowers around them cheering every time a new blossom popped open.

"Well done!"

"That's the way!"

"Hurray for the gorgeous young ones!"

"We knew you could do it!"

"How winsome you are!"

"What loveliness, what pulchritude!" came the voices from all around them.

There was something simply splendid about the flowers in *Wonder*. They each had such fantastic, otherworldly beauty and yet they applauded one another with sincere delight. Not only could the Faultsoms hear the flowers, they could see them in a new way — for they *knew* them, like one knows an old friend: they understood them from the inside out!

The family continued to watch in total absorption as *pollinators* (what Mr. Keeze had called Llopinators) came and went, landing on blossoms all around them, picking up pollen and dispersing the raucous yellow "Llopen" grains at each stop. With delight, the family members relived their flight on the *Bumble Bee* when they were stuck to their pollen buddies. They basked in the memories of their time inside the flower during its reproductive process. Later, they would look back and retrace their experiences and learn more about each of the places they had visited inside the blossom and what was happening there.[1]

As they stared at the flowers skyrocketing up and out of the ground in front of them, they were filled with gladness until they noticed that upon reaching their peak of maturity, the gorgeous petals and lovely green leaves of these blossoms were withering and dropping off. This left their cherished plants quite bare, stripped of everything except a single pod clinging to each stem.

---

1 Dear Reader, we invite you to join the Faultsoms in understanding their puzzling journey by delving into the Wondossary at the end of this book.

"I don't want to see this," Constance reacted bitterly to the fading of the flowers and foliage as if to the loss of a loved one. "It's so sad, why do we need to watch things die?"

Before she could sink into the gloom she felt pooling up within her, she noticed that her forlorn, petal-less plant was trembling ever so slightly. The others, too, noticed this phenomenon and also began to recognize very faint, high-pitched sounds coming from each pod.

As these squealing sounds rose to a crescendo, the flower pods burst open, one by one, shocking the family and practically knocking several of them over. At this, they let out gusts of giggles. Chief and even Charleston were flopping on the ground in glee unable to contain themselves. Constance was snapped out of her melancholy and Chance was trying to figure out how to replicate the explosion. Faye and Frank laughed and smiled.

Once again, *Wonder's* mirth rolled out of the shadows bringing with it waves of rapture and washing away anger, fatigue, and fear. The Faultsoms had just witnessed their seed containers blow up from the *outside* and remembered how they had all exploded out of Madame Yorav (the flower's ovary) from *inside of* her!

Now, laughing and marveling, the Faultsoms watched as the seeds that had exploded out of the ovary pods took to the wind. As their babies fluttered away, the empty flower ovaries that had burst open to set the seeds free, now bent low and deteriorated, yielding themselves to the soil, even as their little ones flew off to begin their life adventures. This act of surrender swallowed up each of the Faultsoms' imaginations as they stood speechless for a long while in the breezy afternoon sunshine.

When the seeds were out of sight, Frank and Faye, Constance, Charleston, Chance, and Chief quietly wandered back to where Mr. Keeze stood, a lump in each of their throats. They were unable to contain the emotions that echoed within them. They gathered in a circle around The Gate Keeper, strangely stirred, but not sure why. They stood together without saying a word, until at long last, Mr. Keeze broke the sacred silence.

CHAPTER 17

Wŏsdim and ꟻntention

"DID YOU *SEE*, MY FRIENDS. DID YOU *SUPPOSE* ANYTHING AT all? Do you *now* understand?" Mr. Keeze queried. When mystified expressions covered each Faultsom face in response, he shook his head and tisk-tisked to himself.

"My, my . . . I can see that only Wosdim will suffice, now." He reached up into the patchwork of keys upon his helmet. "Ah . . . mmmmmm . . . oh . . . where did I put that? My . . . my . . . hooouuum . . ." he muttered.

After rooting around for some time, he found a puzzle piece that had remained entirely hidden among the others, but was possibly the most precious one on his hat. It was covered with gems and ornate scrollwork, and looked quite old and worn. It was shaped like an X although one side was longer than the others. As Mr. Keeze gingerly pulled the key from his helmet, it remained attached by its golden string, which stretched out to the required length. Extending his pinky into the air, he lovingly grasped the key on its longest side between his thumb and forefinger. Lifting it high above his head with great reverence, he whispered breathlessly, announcing to one and all:

"This is the key of Wosdim, for it is Wosdim that we must have now."

Then, reaching as high above him as he could, he stepped up on tiptoe and extended the key straight up. Suddenly, a majestic, glowing red door materialized in the sky above them, hanging flat above their heads. Mr. Keeze, although very short, grew in stature until he could easily slip the key into the empty spot on the front of the door.

Just as he did this, he let go of the key and it whizzed back into its place on his helmet with a *zing*, as the door was flung open, away from them and up into the sky. A refreshing, enlightening presence blew in and shed its glowing light upon Mr. Keeze. He bowed deeply to honor what must have been the presence of this "Wosdim." Then he gathered the Faultsoms in a huddle and began speaking very deliberately to them in a deep and melodious voice:

"Wosdim speaks, my dear Amazings, and now you must pay heed, for Wosdim will speak to you of *Xartief.*" Cocking his head to one side as if to tune into an inaudible voice, he harkened to it and then corrected himself:

"Did I say 'Wosdim?' Did I say 'Xartief?' No, no, no, no . . . I must gather my wits about me, for now is the time when all must come round. Now *Wisdom* will speak to you of *Artifex*, and The All of It All. When you return home, you will need to know *Artifex*. And in order to know *Artifex*, you must receive The Seed."

Artifex? The Faultsoms pondered. Was this the Xartief who was hinted about everywhere they went? Mr. Keeze saw their confusion and confirmed their guesses.

"You must forgive me, my friends. How could it be that I have mixed up the most important word of all? 'Xartief' — indeed not! '*Artifex*', yes! My, my . . ." he said shaking his head at his mistake. "But it is true," he cheered himself, "*Wonder* does have a way of keeping secrets until the time for revelation has come."

Artifex was another very strange word. They still had no idea what it meant, but when they heard it, their hearts leapt with greater anticipation and longing than ever before. As they considered this, Mr. Keeze continued:

"You will find this word, *Artifex*, back in your world, and if you are willing to see it, you will find *The Way of Artifex* hidden in every living thing around you, here and there. If you search and if you see, you will *also* find the heart of *Artifex*, and you will find *The Art* in *The All of It All*. But first, My Amazings, you must receive . . . *The Seed.*"

As he said this, the Faultsoms felt they were awakening to the significance of their journey, and the sensation of this moment was like the feeling of rising out of a long, heavy sleep. He reached down to the ground, pinched an almost imperceptible little speck between his chubby fingers, and held it up before them.

"Let *The Seed* tell us the story of *The Art* -- *The Intention* of *The All of It All*," he began. "Just as *The Seed* must be buried in the earth, so it must also be planted in you if it is to awaken. It must be buried in the dark place of mystery, yes, in the dust. Once it is received here, its new life is aroused by soil and warmth and moisture. But always, to know and to understand *Artifex* and *The Art* in everything, you must receive *The Seed*; there is no other way.

"Never forget that a seed is a wee living thing. Inside its shell, it carries the miracle of *Generation*. This is the *Way of Artifex*, the way of Knight seeking Bride. The way of the *He and She* co-mingled, surrendering themselves. They are incomplete without each other and without *The Intention*.

"Let us marvel at the zealous, passionate bravery and vitality of The Knight (The He) who relentlessly seeks after the beauteous Bride (The She) to pour himself into her. And my, The Bride, what valor and bravery she displays! Far from being weak or passive, she will grow to her fullness and then give herself utterly to launch the next generation of life into the unknown. This is love in its wholeness! And what of The Knight and Bride as they abandon themselves to *The Intention*? Together they are matured and completed in the breathtaking splendor of the joyous and extravagant bloom that results from their union."

Mr. Keeze now blew upon the seed between his fingers, releasing it from his grasp. He watched it flutter away.

"Look about you, my friends, here . . ." The Gate Keeper bent down and gently cupped a spectacularly gorgeous blossom in the palms of his hands.

"Here inside this exquisite blossom, with its intoxicating fragrance, lies the mystery of *The Intention* to which The Knight and Bride, *The He and She,* surrender themselves. They teach us that pleasure must never be an end in itself. Pleasure's fullness nourishes others and brings forth new life. The very purpose of the flower is to reproduce new life. Its fragrance, shape, and color invite the

Llopinator . . . no, ahh . . . your word is *Pollinator* . . . to come and be nourished. And *The Pollinator* fulfills *The Intention* — its purpose, by carrying the pollen to its destiny — the destiny of *Generation* — the Generation, the creation of a seedling. As with the purpose of all pleasures, you must understand that the delights of the flower are not solely to thrill and please those who enjoy it. No, these ecstasies are always and forever entwined with *The Intention* of nourishing others and bringing forth new life. And each of *you* are the result of the *life-giving joinings of a He and She.* You are the Amazelings that have come of their loving *Generations*."

Mr. Keeze nodded at Faye and Frank and let his words sink in as he watched *Wisdom's* light dawn upon each Faultsom brow and leave her kiss. After a few moments, he spoke again:

"Do you now see, my dear friends, that in the end, the flower surrenders itself and all its beauty in order to make a way for its precious seeds to be cast forth upon the wind? The blossom gives up its glories and pleasures to make a way for its babies to be planted in the earth. These in turn carry *The Art of The Intention* — *The Way of Artifex.* Seeds grow and bloom and nourish new life. *Artifex Be Extolled!*"

As he said this, each Faultsom felt themselves resonate with every flower waving in the endless fields that encompassed them. They entire family reverberated, with a passionate cry:

"*Artifex Be Extolled, indeed!*"

After a moment of reflection, Mr. Keeze's eyes darkened sharply and then dimmed with a look of sorrow.

"In your world, many have not known of *The Intention* — the purpose in *The All of It All.* They have not known *The Ardor of Artifex* truly expressed in Knight and Bride. Even the flowers in your world understand what people have forgotten: that true love is only known in complete surrender to selfless intentions. Without this selfless love, many hearts in your world, though they survive, are never truly awakened to true life."

"Papa!" Chief cried as he sidled up to his Dad and reached his arms up. "What ith he talking about? What ith *The Ardor of Artifeth* and all that thtuff?"

Frank picked up his youngest son and looked into his freckled face:

"Well, buddy, I think Mr. Keeze means that there is a plan of love inside of everything . . . a purpose . . . and he is saying that we can find it in each seed."

"Well, I knew *that*, Papa. Thath tho obvioth. Doethn't everyone know that?"

Frank chuckled and squeezed Chief's face up close to his own, as they turned their attention back to The Gate Keeper.

"No, my little Amazeling, not everyone understands this. Many will never receive *The Seed*; many will never surrender themselves to *The Intention*, but will hoard lifeless pleasures and seek to generate their own empty plans. True life and love never come of this.

"All of *Wonder* wonders at such sad goings-on in your world. Some of those who do not know *The Ardor of Artifex* seek to fill the void with empty, selfish pleasure and personal fulfillment. Others desire to stamp their own likenesses, whims, and desires upon one another. These things can only produce tragic, hollow results, and create shallow, puppet-like people who do not nurture the growth of true selfless Intention and Purpose."

Faye and Frank nodded their heads, recalling the vacant look in the eyes of so many of the kids they saw coming home each day from The Grown-Up Factory. Right then and there, they knew that even though it would cost them everything, they would never stop fighting for their family to know *Wonder*'s Intention. And in this *Purpose*, maybe one day, they would all know *The Ardor* of this *Artifex*, which was somehow hidden in *The All of It All*.

Thinking out loud, Faye ventured:

"I know what you are saying is real, but is there hope for our world?"

"My slocks and sippers . . . no . . . ah . . . here it is . . . my *socks and slippers*! Of course there is hope! Dear friends, here is the marvelous secret hidden in every *Seed of Wonder*: Even when humans are not championed by selfless love, even when you fail each other, *The Intention of Artifex* is still buried in the soil of each life. When *The*

Seed penetrates even the most forsaken of hearts, it awakens. So, in *The Seed*, there is *Hope*."

At this, The Gate Keeper approached each member of the family, one at a time. Starting with Frank and then Faye and afterward, moving to each child, he stopped and paused, gripped their hands in his, and poured a twinkle's worth of his joyous gaze into each Faultsom's heart. As he did this, Frank, Faye, Constance, Charleston, Chance, and Chief were stilled with quiet assurance, feeling waves of pure love flow down upon them through the majestic red door that hovered and opened in the sky. It flowed through Mr. Keeze as he whispered a special secret into the ear of each family member. Standing on his tiptoes, he spoke softly to Faye:

"My Dear, do you know who you are . . . ?"

As he continued, Faye felt that his words carried weight, yet they drifted away on a the breath of a zephyr, making them inaudible to anyone else. Faye's brow furrowed as she tried to make out their significance.

To Constance he whispered, "You have the heart of the valorous Bride and the *Intention* of the passionate Knight is pursuing you. *Generation* awaits you. You are brave and strong and you carry a great *Purpose* — to scatter the *Wonder* of new life into your world through your strength, beauty, and fragrance. Receive *The Ardor of Artifex* and give *this* love to the forsaken."

What he said to each of the others may not be revealed at this time, Dear Reader, but let it be said that Mr. Keeze's words swept the remaining cobwebs from their minds and shooed the lingering fears from their souls. When he had finished, he gave them one more admonishment:

"As you return, my dear ones, I leave you with these Seeds. Receive them and they will grow. They will bring the hope of *Generation* into your world."

"But my friends, beware the thorns and darts of *The Shadowlands*! You will pass through dim places as you return. But remember, there is always hope."

At this, he clicked his heels together, wiped a tear from his eye, bowed deeply, and waved goodbye.

As the air around them began to swim and they faded from his presence, the Faultsoms caught one last glance of The Gate Keeper standing with his hand upon his heart. From a distance they heard his deep and melodious voice echoing:

"Receive The Seeds . . . receeeeeeiiiiive The Seeeeedddss!"

CHAPTER 18

The Shadowlands

THEY WERE TRANSMIGRATING, FILTERING IN AND OUT OF spaces and pathways as if moving through hidden doors in a fun-house maze. Penetrating layers of time and dimension, the voyagers felt themselves sinking down, deeper and deeper, into an atmosphere that grew heavier and darker with each passing moment. There were flashes of light and cloudy mists through which they traveled toward their inevitable destination — a destination that they desperately wished they would never have to reach. The Faultsoms were aware of each sensation as they absorbed the impact of the words Mr. Keeze had whispered into their ears. His *Seeds* carried a weight that penetrated their consciousness, imparting strength to their hearts. They were comforted by what he had said, that is, until they began to feel a shift in the atmosphere. Their journey was taking them through a very scary place which was thick with shadows and dark light. Sensing danger mounting all around them, the unsuspecting Faultsoms felt as though they would suffocate in the dread that was quickly engulfing them.

"Heeere *they* commme! Thossse ssssickening *Wwwon-der-erssss!*" A brittle, hissing voice spit the words out with such disgust as though it was choking on the gall of its own hatred.

"It isss farrr worsssseee than we antisss-ipated!" A spying scout screeched in revulsion, alarming many others who had hidden themselves in the shadows.

"The He and She and the sssspppawn of *their* Generationssss have . . . Sseedsssss!"

Now the entire cohort was in full battle alert. Their commander shrieked:

"They musssst be neutralizzzed before it'ssss too late. The Pressscribed Order musssst not be quessstioned!"

Razor-sharp shafts and thorns were unsheathed and aimed with chilling accuracy. Deadly in their subtlety, these weapons were cunningly designed to leave wounds that would go undetected. Each one inflicted just enough discomfort to penetrate its victim and unleash an insidious flow of refined destruction, but never produced enough pain to actually reveal the true nature of its immense threat. A chill wind blew upon the Faultsoms now, and mocking hisses teased their thoughts.

"Ow! What was that?" Chance was assaulted by a stab at his heel.

"Yikths, Mama . . . thomething jutht bit me on the leg! Like a huge mothquito . . . no fair!" Chief was incensed at the attack.

"Sheesh! What is this?" Charleston felt a scratch across his arm leaving an abrasion of some sort.

They were now being propelled quickly as if to get them out of this dim and dreadful region as soon as possible. More darkness, and more hissing surrounded them.

"Something sharp pricked my forehead, Mom." Constance cried out.

"I feel tho prickly!" Chance yelled.

Sensing the growing danger, the unsuspecting travelers felt as though they would suffocate in the dread that was quickly engulfing them. Sizzling and sputtering sounds pierced the air as the darts found their marks and the thorns and brambles about them scratched their fragile flesh. Each prick implanted poisonous invading thoughts that would soon grow to choke out all opposition.

"You've been trrrriccckked!"

"This is jusssst a fantasssssy."

"You're Forssssaken."

"It'ssss all your fault . . ."

Creepy voices whispered cruel thoughts, gleefully inflicting their venomous little torments. Frank felt something pierce him between the shoulder blades. Faye felt a jab just under her rib cage.

"This must be 'The Shadowlands'!" Chance shouted.

"Ith tho creepy!" Chief wailed.

"I'm afraid!" Constance cried.

Frank had an inspiration:

"The Seeds! Everyone, Mr. Keeze said, 'Receive The Seeds'!" Frank boomed. "Focus on what Mr. Keeze said . . . think about what he told you!"

Faye turned The Gate Keeper's words over and over in her head as she plummeted through the shadows.

"Dare to *Wonder* . . . To find *Artifex* is to be found," Mr. Keeze had whispered to her. But spewing from the darkness was an acrimonious voice opposing her.

"It'ssss all your fault, Mrsss. *Fault*ssssom . . . you have failed . . . "

Constance found herself listening to an eerie voice, as she tried to remember what Mr. Keeze had told her.

"Forssssakennn. Alonnne. You are neverrrr enoughhhh."

Constance was chilled to the bone as the words penetrated.

"It'sss all a myth . . . You are too ssssmart to be trapped in this fantassssyyyyyy . . ." The voice trailed off into the distance.

"Don't be fooled by their delusionssss . . . There issss no Purposssseee."

Cheering with glee, the attackers retreated into the periphery, gloating over the impact of their warcraft. Victory was surely at hand. If these meddlesome interlopers did not resist, they would soon drift into acquiescence. Watching with evil anticipation, the assailants were thrilled to see their victims succumbing to a lethal mixture of doubt, fear, and depression.

"Successssss!" came the jubilant hisses. They were certain they would prevail.

Suddenly, a string of their curses filled the atmosphere for their evil assault was somehow being countervailed. So it was, for when the Faultsoms focused on their Seed Secrets the pain inflicted on them would diminish, and the hope in them would brighten. But as they passed through the shadows and descended into their own world, they each had to fight hard to keep from being overwhelmed by the panic and growing feeling of depression that assaulted them on every side. Faye and Constance felt their energy draining away. It was so difficult to resist the dark voices.

The wicked watchers were now observing with dread. The He and his boy-spawn were putting up a fight! With them victory could not be assured. At least not, yet. But the She and the girl-spawn were another matter. They had failed to resist.

Just when the Faultsoms thought their trial would never end, the family heard a happy, funny sound in the distance. What could *that* be? Why, it was the echoing of The Song! What a relief! It cut through the dark thicket they were traversing and vibrated in the air, creating a welcoming sonic landing pad for them. They were actually entering back into those last moments outside their home when they had burst out into that silly singing! They could even hear their own voices rising up from beneath them, and they joined in singing with themselves as their feet touched the ground and their bodies gained substance. Cornelius, their hound dog, was still barking wildly and running back and forth when they became visible again to The Well Being Officers, who were still standing on the sidewalk, absolutely flabbergasted.

With effervescent and utterly ridiculous good humor — especially in light of what they were still facing — the Faultsoms stood together bellowing that insidiously optimistic song — laughing and crying. Now they sang it with new words:

> We are Jolly Jaunty Voy'gers!
> A *returning* delegation
> For we've found our happy hearts
> And sing for joy with admiration
> Of the *Wondrous* seeds and secrets
> That *deserve* our cogitation.
> So there's hope enough in every heart
> To change this rotten situation!

CHAPTER 19

Overcoming The POO

THERE THEY WERE, IN FRONT OF THEIR DUMBLE STREET home, hugging each other and laughing and chattering incessantly like Llopens! Chance noticed that their banter carried a familiar quality to it and shouted above the noisy voices:

"Hey, Ho, there, family! Here we are — the natty, nattering Faultsoms!"

Recognizing the familiarity of their energetic jabbering, Charleston giggled:

"Ever the excitable chaps, aren't we?"

"Yeth! Leths Down and Dig!" Chief chimed in.

"Yeah, you guys *do* sound like those annoying little fuzzballs . . ." Constance had a bit of a snarky tone in her voice, but then she cracked a good-humored grin.

Faye and Frank looked on, smiling as silly "pollen-esian" sayings bubbled up and out of their lips as well. This strange embodiment in their midst of their histamine-provoking friends was oddly reassuring, as the Well Being Officers who were still there, had overcome some of their shock and were now closing in around them.

As the officials approached to seize the children from their parents, they walked into the middle of the Faultsoms' uproarious, Llopen-y yakking, and suddenly started to sneeze! They sneezed and sneezed and could not stop! With their eyes watering like sprinklers and their noses stuffed up like cocktail olives, the officers were quite incapacitated. They were pretty perturbed and perfectly pitiful.

It was then that it began to dawn upon members of the family that something from *Wonder* was breaking into their world! It was as if they had brought the Llopens back to Dumble Street, or maybe they had paved the way for the WBOs to encounter *Wonder's* whacky goings-on.

A lightbulb turned on inside Chance's head and he shouted out.

"Wow, guys! This is *too* weird. I just had this idea: What if stuff that happened in *Wonder* can happen *here* somehow?"

"Yes . . . " Charleston mused, "Makes one consider the possibilities. Perhaps there are other experiences we can import from *Wonder* into our realm now that we have returned."

"Cool! I'm going to try it . . . thith ith going to be *my favorite part of the job, thith ith!*" Chief exulted as he quoted Mr. Keeze.

Giving each other a knowing look, the boys clapped high fives, hugged their sister and parents, grabbed their bags, and deposited themselves in the vehicles assigned to take them away from home. This they did, mischievously, jabbering like Llopens while the deputies continued to sneeze, wiping their watery eyes and blowing their noses on their coat sleeves.

Constance, too, ran to give everyone a last kiss, laughing at her brothers as a wave of hope rose in her heart. Moments later, however, she felt a jab in the middle of her back and noticed a faint hissing sound behind her as she ducked into the waiting car. She turned to see where this came from, but saw nothing. Dismissing this as just being in her imagination, she was determined to shake the dark feelings.

Faye and Frank waved goodbye. How was it they could be so sad and yet so hopeful, so concerned and yet so calm all at the same time? But this is how they felt. So, they shouted their "I love you's," surrendered their kids to an unknown future, and walked back into their forlorn old house, arm in arm, with faithful Cornelius trailing along, quite confused.

As determined by the State, Constance, Chance, Charleston, and Chief were sent to separate temporary care facilities until they could complete a Social Re-Alignment Program (or SyRAP, as they came to call it). Although the kids attended SyRAP sessions with program counselors assigned to reorder their thoughts and beliefs, they seemed, for the most part, to remain the irrepressibly curious and ebullient kids they had been before.

To the degree that they learned to be absorbed in *Wonder*, they were more or less impervious to the effects of the sappy, sickening, SyRAP'y seminars. These were very dark and confusing times, to be sure, but the realignment curriculum didn't compete well with the curious clues they began to discover around them when they looked closely. These clues hinted at *Artifex* and *The Intention* in *The All of It All*.

Even when they were told that they needed to give up the outdated, antisocial, and unscientific notions they had grown up with, the Faultsom kids had available to them the sound, sights, and sensations of *Wonder* — if they chose to focus on *that dimension*.

During times when they felt lonely, isolated, or anxious they would feel the sting of the wounds they had received as they descended through The Shadowlands. Doubt, fear, and emptiness would creep over them and fill their thoughts with cynical skepticism and bitterness. Until, that is, they chose to remember and cherish the words The Gate Keeper had whispered in their ears.

Back home, rambling around their empty Dumble Street house with Corneilus, and aching most terribly for their children, Frank and Faye clung to their reminiscences of *Wonder*.

Faye was frequently visited by fear in the night hours as she worried about her kids. Always, when this happened, she felt a pain hit her under her rib cage as her thoughts unraveled. What if her kids were harmed? She had no way to protect them or help them. Awful outcomes flooded her mind. The kids were off in those state facilities under the control of people whose job it was to reprogram them. If it weren't for her and her wild ideas and crazy pursuits, maybe things would be different. Why did she always insist on pushing the envelope? Why couldn't she just back off and let Frank take the lead in these things? That would have been safer. Maybe then they could have all just fit it with everybody else and stayed out of trouble.

"But no," she chided herself, "you always have to let your passions run wild. Now look where that has led us!"

Then Faye would long for the happy light in *Wonder* and try to recall the special words Mr. Keeze had spoken to her, but over time those words grew very faint in her memory.

Sometimes both Frank and Faye felt like they were free-falling into the darkness, and ti was then that Frank would comfort his wife by reminding her of their exhilarating drop inside of the *Wonderous* tunnelslide, which they later learned was a pollen tube making its way down the flower stem and into its ovary.

Recalling their thrilling descent, the couple would remember they had been screaming, just like kids, at the top of their lungs in sheer joy, as they simply *trusted*. Inside the memory of being in that pollen tube as it reached relentlessly into the darkness, Faye and Frank could learn to trust again when they thought of the glowing pollen cells guiding them to the brink of a continuing cliff, upon a living conduit that never let them fall. Somehow, back in their own world, on the brink of a seemingly never-ending precipice, a sense of *Purpose* and peace offered itself to them. Perhaps there was *Intention* in all of this, and so they *wondered*. Would their kids find their way in the dark, just as the Knight and Squire had? Hope whispered from inside them.

"Yes, even in this . . . "

And it was true. The kids did find their way somehow, and the boys helped others find their way as well. Charleston, Chance, and Chief met other outliers who did not fit in with The Prescribed Order.

They sometimes overheard the officials talking about how trouble-some it was when children did not cooperate with "The Prescribed Order Operation," and although the boys did not know what this plan was, they called it The POO, and that's just what it was like. To them, The POO was not at all like the selfless *Intention* of *Artifex*.

Charleston would lie awake at night and ruminate on this, recalling what Mr. Keeze had said to them all just before he said goodbye:

"Those who do not know *The Ardor of Artifex* desire to stamp their own likenesses, whims, and desires upon one another."

Could it be that The Gatekeeper was talking about things like The POO? As Charleston pondered this, he also considered the hints about *Artifex* which he was discovering, even in this most unlikely of places.

Even when The WBOs were focused on dismantling the kids' belief in *Wonder*, if the Faultsom fledglings really looked for it, it was obvious to them that *Intention* was everywhere. Chance and Charleston also began to understand that things went terribly wrong when this *Intention* was thwarted, and the result was ugly. This filled them all the more with determination to search out the selfless purpose of *Artifex*.

As they persevered through The SyRAP, the boys discovered that replaying their adventures in *Wonder* really did affect those around them. One time, Chance took off into the ozone, reliving every moment of his breathless *flight* on Mistress Bublem Eeb and the G-forces he experienced. When he did this, his counselor suddenly became extremely dizzy and nauseous and had to leave the room to find a toilet, right in the middle of his attempt to convince Chance that none of his multidimensional fantasies were real.

Chance also had enormous fun singing The Song to his new friends in the facility. When they were depressed, angry, or afraid, it was really something to watch how The Song lifted spirits and imparted a delicious feeling of silliness and expectancy, like something tremendous could be just around the corner:

Dear Inmates, Friends, and Scallywags,
Was it something that we ate
That made us so uncouth, unkind,
Unable to appreciate
All that lies before us
In the fabric of our days?
Our attitudes are stinky and
We'd better change our ways.

Dear Pals and Rug Rat Sillies
We're just moments from relief
Or days and days from happiness
'f we wallow in our grief.
Let's look for all the clues and hints
Despite those who oppose it.
Wonder's world is near, my friends,
For all who will suppose it!

Noticing how The Song had begun to change things for his friends, Chance tried an experiment. He tried singing it quietly when his SyRAP Directors were particularly overbearing:

You Dastardly Despoilers
You do need this so
Despite the things you say and do
And the things you think you know.
Wonder knows what's best for you
Even if you hate it.
Give up *The* nasty rotten *Plan*
So trouble is abated.

Despite the domineering demeanor of these grown-ups, when The Song began to fill the atmosphere, the facilitators would take on a petulant, childlike quality and find themselves unhappy with the status quo, clearly longing for something they told the kids wasn't real. Sensing this, The Songsters would smile knowingly at each other.

Charleston discovered that what most excited his sensibilities was his memory of the energy, light, and music of *The Generation*. He would absorb this into himself and could feel it echoing in his heart and flowing out of him. It was as though his soul was the soundboard that made *Wonder* reverberate in the natural world.

When this happened, the hardened, lonely, and confused kids around him would become quiet and thoughtful. Tears would sometimes well up in their eyes as their hearts were filled with unfamiliar thoughts of pure love giving itself completely to bring forth and nurture new life. They felt the reality of a truly selfless love nurturing even *them*.

Then there was Chief. During the endless retraining classes, he daydreamed constantly about his family's trip to *Wonder*. Between his classes, he spent his time imagining new places he might visit in *Wonder* and regaling his classmates with stories. He and his friends figured out early on that it was best to go along with the goofy stuff the grown-ups taught them during the day, but at night, when they all settled down in the bunkhouse, they rejoiced in their secret *Wonder Club* meetings, during which the kids peppered Chief with questions about his adventures.

As he recounted the tales, the kids could feel a kind of portal open up in the atmosphere around them and they were transported into the middle of the scenes Chief described. The members of the *Wonder Club* solemnly vowed that when they returned home they would search until they found this mysterious *Artifex*, who was in *The All of It All*.

While he kept a fairly low profile — which was no small achievement for Chief who wanted to run the show in pretty much every setting — The WBOs had their suspicions about his progress. One afternoon, near the end of The SyRAP seminars, the plucky little seven-year-old was called in for evaluation by the realignment team, chaired by none other than Ms. Imperia Beasley! The Developmental Well-Being and Life Skills Assessment experts were meeting to determine if Chief was going to need more remediation in order to turn his mind away from his family's backward notions and deficient educational methods.

It was a humid afternoon when Chief's SyRAP counselor walked him into the conference room of the Well-Being Center and brought him before a group of very uncomfortable-looking grown-ups. The cooling unit in the building was not working and the air was quite moist and stuffy. Ms. Beasley sat in a swivel chair in the middle of the room wearing a blouse of large yellow and black stripes that seemed to be an attempt to compensate for her overbearing, dictatorial countenance. But no colorful clothes could make her look at all pleasant.

Swiveling in a grandiose fashion to face the members of the committee, she began the meeting.

"Good morning, everyone. Today we will review one of the cases from that very disconcerting state of affairs we encountered in the vicinity of The Center for Child Development and Life Preparation number 1557. The officials of The Developmental Well-Being and Life Skills Assessment Committee (The DoWLSAC) investigated the situation and determined that the unstructured educational style of the Faultsom family was wholly inadequate in preparing their children for real-world workforce demands. Furthermore, the committee was most concerned about the bizarre and delusional experiences that Mr. and Mrs. Faultsom were encouraging their children to indulge in.

"We are here today to determine if this child, Conrad Carlisle Faultsom, has been sufficiently realigned with The Prescribed Order."

With a supercilious swoosh, Ms. Beasley swiveled around to face Chief, who was standing with his counselor a few feet away from her. Addressing him with a forced smile and a sappy sweet tone of voice, she spoke:

"Come here, Conrad, you musn't be afraid. I simply want to ask you some questions to see how you have enjoyed your time here at Camp Common Kid."

At this, she motioned for Chief to step forward and stand right in front of her.

"Closer, young man, come here and stand right next to me so I can see your bright little face nice and close up." Chief felt himself bristle at the thought of coming so close to Ms. Beasley, but obeyed dutifully.

"Now, please tell us what you've learned here about how to bring your new Common Kid values back home to your family. How can you help your parents understand the New World ways?"

The hot, damp air in the room made Chief feel woozy, but worse than that, he was bowled over by Ms. Beasley's horrific halitosis. Her breath was disgusting! It smelled something like stale coffee, dead fish, and stinky cheese. Chief involuntarily threw his hands up in front of his nose and mouth, and took a step back, while a couple of the grown-ups on the committee unsuccessfully attempted to stifle their amusement, much to Ms. Beasley's dismay.

The Beasley (as some members of the committee called her privately) pulled Chief's hands away from his face, yanking him closer and addressing him again, this time with a higher-pitched tone.

"Conrad, we are waiting to hear your ins-*hi*-ghts."

She exhaled as she said it, discharging more of her noxious vapor, causing Chief to lurch away from her and cover his nose and mouth again. A scathing scowl overtook The Beasley's face. Chief's reaction seemed to her to be an act of defiance, which increased her determination to elicit answers from the youngest Faultsom.

Now, Chief knew he was really in trouble, and mustering up his imagination, he went back into *Wonder*. He was desperately searching his memories for something that would be helpful in this particular situation, just as The Beasley got out of her chair and bent down directly in front of him. She craned her neck forward until her face was within inches of his and took a breath, preparing to speak again.

The fragrance! That was it! Chief could remember the enormously pleasing aroma that the flowers in *Wonder* emitted to lure the pollinators to their petals. Chief's brain recalled the sweet musky incense as The Beasley's newly exhaled breath headed toward his nostrils. Just in time, the "scent had been sent," and its floral bouquet blocked The Beasley's odor! More surprisingly, *she* caught a whiff of that glorious fragrance, too. As it hit her olfactory nerve, her eyes widened and her head began to spin slightly, distracting her momentarily. Refocusing with some effort, the head of The DoWLSAC was determined to exert control again.

"Conrad Carlisle *Faultsom*, I must insist that you tell us what you've learned about the New World ways and why myth and fancy are *sooo* unhoopful."

Noticing that Ms. Beasley was also affected by the flower power he was immersing himself in, Chief grinned at her as he doubled down on his *Wondering*. Now, he not only called forth the scent of the flowers but focused intently on the "Tenarc" that Mistress Eeb loved so much. He recalled her happy humming as she sucked in the honeyed *nectar* from *Wonder*'s floral smorgasbord. Chief began to hum right along with her. Ignoring Ms. Beasley's questions, he just hummed out loud as if he were a Bumble Bee having a luscious sweet drink:

"Mmmmmm-mmmm, hummmmmm a hummmy hummm . . . "

My, how this infuriated The Beasley! There was little Chief humming away, now immune to her breath and her questions as he stared off into the distance with an enchanting little smile lighting up his freckled cheeks. He just stood there enjoying a loopy feeling in his head that made him snort and titter.

That was it! Ms. Imperia Beasley's calm and controlled exterior cracked, causing her comrades on the committee no small amount of alarm. The Beasley boiled over and sort of shrieked as she stood up.

"Let the committee note that this child must not be allowed to upset The Prescribed Order!"

As she carried on, her voice became even more brittle and ominous. What had happened to their composed, caring, and reasonable chairwoman? A provocative thought crossed the committee members' minds: *Could it be that Ms. Beasley was unsuited for her duties?* Just as this possibility occurred to them, it hit her.

Ms. Imperia Beasley was sloshed. Potted. Plastered. Drunk as a skunk.

Walking toward the committee members, she listed to the left and then to the right, winding back and forth across the room. Realizing she was losing her grip on things, she threw her shoulders back most comically and attempted to right her path. Struggling to speak with an authoritative air, she babbled:

"Ladies and Gemimines, I am soooo shouure you can all now suurrrmiiiizze cluurrly that this child mustsst be mee-reediated fruther. He must confrom to the scre-pribed dddorder."

As she said this, a ridiculous grin overcame her usually taught facial features, and she began to chuckle.

"Order?" She tooted out quizzically . . . "who knows what *that* izzz anywayzzz? Order schmoorder! Doesn't aaanywahone ever have annyy fun anymooore?" she slurred. "I'm sooo tired of being so uptooty — and uptight."

She pulled her overcompensatingly colorful blouse out of her skirt and opened the top button as she hiccupped.

"Izzzit hot in here?"

The committee watched incredulously as Ms. Beasley began to hum and flit around the room, with her eyes closed.

"Hmmmm. I am floating! This is marvelllll-ouuuzzzzzz. Flitty, flitty here and flitty floatty there. I'm a Bee! Buzzy buzzzzzz buzzz . . . "

Ms. Beasley began to wave her hands very quickly as if they were bee's wings. There was no stopping her now.

"I alwaaayzzz kneeew I could flyyyyy . . . ever since I was gittle lirl. But," she choked up, "No one believe-ded me . . . and then, they told me I wasn't allowed to believe in anything — truly wonderful — ever again."

Her words trailed off and she began to cry. Collapsing on the floor near Chief, she sat in a heap, sniveling and buzzing to herself. He ran over to her and threw his arms around her, humming into her ear and singing quietly.

"Mith Thargent! The *Wonder* door ith open . . . leth's leave this detholathunnnnnn . . . "

It was then that Chief was quickly escorted from the room and, as The Committee Members would admit to one another later, a bizarre thing occurred: Ms. Imperia Beasley looked as if she were fading away!

What happened to Ms. Beasley may never be fully known to us, but suffice it to say she never quite regained her composure or the esteem she once possessed in the eyes of The Committee Members and DoWLSAC officials. In fact, her drunken behavior before the officials that fateful day led to the reopening of the Faultsom family case.

It became evident then, that Ms. Beasley was the primary force behind the State's decision to remove the Faultsom children from the family home and enroll them in the Social Re-Alignment Program. Since Ms. Beasley could no longer be considered trustworthy, the officials felt her involvement in this matter was a liability. Deciding to avoid any further embarrassment, they sent the Faultsom children home. They further determined to leave this family, with their strange ways, to themselves for the foreseeable future. The officials further noted that the more they endeavored to impress The POO upon these children, the more it had the opposite effect upon the Faultsom boys and their peers in the SyRAP. As a whole, this family's case was going to be too much trouble to deal with.

So it was that, in the springtime a little less than a year after the fateful garden party, Constance, Charleston, Chance, and Chief were returned to Dumble Street and into the waiting arms of their parents and the paws of their slobbering dog. The boys recounted story after story to their thankful parents about how they had managed to survive, and even thrive, in hostile territory. And the household was once again convulsing with their boyish exuberance.

Constance's journey through the Social Re-Alignment Program was of a different sort from that of her brothers. She carried the words of The Gate Keeper inside her somewhere, and it comforted and encouraged her when she focused on them. However, the longer she was in The S'RAP, the more The Seed planted by The Gate Keeper was overshadowed by grim, hissing, brambly barbs invading her mind. They grew up inside her and wrapped themselves around her heart.

At times, she recalled *Wonder* and it was like a breath of fresh air, but then it seemed just out of reach, like a far too distant memory. As her weeks in the program went by, *Wonder* seemed to her to be more and more like some kind of nursery story her mother had told her years before. She became increasingly skeptical, isolated, and desolate, and she felt that no silly fairy tale would make things better. She concluded that she was on her own to deal with the stark realities of the world outside of her family home.

A strange pain often jabbed her in the back, and when it did, she could almost hear a hissing voice in her head. At these times she felt particularly alone and dejected as she bitterly considered how selfish and self-involved her parents were. What a disservice they had done to her and her brothers by immersing them in the family delusion! And Mom, well, *she* had really been the pushy one, pressuring them to accept her illusions and take part in her trippy excursions. And Dad, well *he* shouldn't have let her do that to them. Could Constance ever really trust either one of them again?

In the Social Re-Alignment program, the facilitators helped her see how logic and reason forbade belief in *Wonder* and the like. Constance was now beginning to realize how important it was for everyone to work together to bring about The Plan. Even if it went against her creative intuition, she grew to believe that this was the best thing for everyone. People had to be on the same page and play their role in The Prescribed Order. Things in the real world were chaotic, out of control, and unfair. But her counselor assured her that The Leaders had a good plan and she could help. Thankfully, being in The SyRAP had opened her mind, and she would do her part.

Still, night after night, Constance was troubled by a mysterious dream. As she drifted off into the deepest regions of slumber, she would rise out of her body, floating over a peculiar- looking little man who lay sleeping on the floor inside a glowing chamber and, she would begin to dance.

CHAPTER 20

Mrs. Amazing and The Seed

FAYE FAULTSOM HAD BEEN LOOKING BACK. HER JOURNEY began abruptly on that tearful and troubling evening when Constance drove off, leaving her mother alone to make sense of her daughter's painful declaration of disbelief. Faye's recollections and rehearsals over the months since then had taken her through the long dark winter of her family's adventures and travails, and back through her daughter's journey away from home.

She finally came to the end of her wanderings one day as she stood at her kitchen sink overlooking the unfurling foliage of her early summer garden. She was glad to have the house to herself that afternoon, for she was brimming over with conflicting thoughts and emotions.

Just as the family's drafty vintage home shuddered during stormy outbursts of foul weather but still managed to stay firmly planted on Dumble Street, so the Faultsom family had been deeply shaken by their own tornado of trouble but had managed to survive the howling onslaught against them and their unconventional way of life.

There was fallout, to be sure, but at least Frank and Faye had stood rooted together. This had resulted in the growth of new possibilities unfolding before them, while at the same time they watched other ones die.

In the end, Faye's boundless passion and creativity could not be stopped. She would always find a way to explore the promise of a new horizon. Thankfully, Faye knew that her faulterings and foibles, along with her inevitable mothering malfunctions, were balanced by Frank's kindness, practicality, and wisdom. And she, in turn, gave him the jump-start he often needed to keep his head out of The PP (Peerless Pencil) by finding ways to help him awaken his own fearless and slightly goofy "inner" Faultsom. For this and so much more, he treasured her and she honored him with warmth that overflowed her heart and hopes. They both had their failings, but together they made up much more than the sum of their parts. Opening their arms to an enlarging circle of curious wanderers, their Dumble Street oasis had become a place where sojourners like themselves could find a bit of *Wonder*.

Their sons, though they had endured many a searing doubt and daunting struggle, returned from their time in The SiRAP with more imagination in their souls than their parents could have thought possible. Charleston reentered the Faultsom orbit with the ability to launch into deep space at a moment's notice. He flew off into dimensions that his parents could never reach, but he would, in due season, gravitate back to earth, bringing with him the treasures he gathered from the far reaches of the galaxies he explored in his search for *Artifex*.

His cello was his closest traveling companion on these journeys into the far and near, and it became his favored method of communicating the things he discovered. He found enjoyment in his role in their community orchestra and, in his teenage years, rose up the ranks as a cellist of note. He also began to compose and perform music of such an ethereal quality that it never failed to have a *Wonderous* effect upon those who listened to it. They found themselves awakened to another dimension and floating in a supernal sweetness that flowed out of Charleston's musings. Frustratingly, however, he tended to be disconnected from day-to-day life, for he was ever the introspective voyager. It was quite an accomplishment that he stayed integrated into the fabric of the family, making his unique contributions to the Faultsom frenzy.

Chance was as high-spirited and unpredictable as ever. Always one to keep things interesting, he became obsessed with creating a host of mind-bending blueprints and inventions. Among them were his prototypes for a self-elongating slide and a fusion-energy reactor. He was determined to bring the possibilities of *Wonder* into this world. His friends, a rather odd and nerdy group of kids, poured in and out of the house carrying all sort of gadgets and gizmos as they rattled on about velocity, friction, resistance, inter-dimensional travel, and strategy battle games. Their brains were ignited by ideas and excitement which seemed to flow in from another realm and into the Faultsom basement — as Chance lit the wicks.

Chief organized a *Wonder Club* for interested neighborhood buddies. The Dumble Street backyard clubhouse became a place of refuge and exploration for many a misfit. They would show up as if drawn by the scent of something delicious in the atmosphere. Sometimes they were impelled to investigate the often over-the-top, pollen-like Faultsom energy and wound up encouraged by them to take a thrilling slide into the unknown. When energies were running at their peak voluminosity, there was something about the Faultsom boys' and their folks' oddly funny and yet profound conversations that were irresistible . . . exhausting, but irresistible.

Much can be said, and should be written about the supernatural safaris, misadventures, dilemmas, and victories of *all* The Knights Faultsom, but for now let it be known that, through the years, many perilous and *Wonderful* doors were opened for these young men as they overcame the thorns and darts of The Shadowlands and continued their search for *Artifex* in *The All of It All*. And let it be duly noted that these explorers discovered this most rare and perplexing word, *Artifex*, does indeed have a singularly grand and important meaning in our world.[2]

The Ladies Faultsom had a very different journey. The road of Constance's return to the house was quite a bumpy one. The eldest Faultsom offspring found herself withdrawing from the family in general, and from her mother in particular, spending more and more time with a set of friends she made while in the program.

Faye could feel Constance slipping away but hoped it was just a phase. She tried repeatedly, bumbling in her attempts to draw Constance back into the fold. This often only succeeded in worsening the growing rift between Constance and the family. Frank was sometimes able to diffuse the rising tensions, but his daughter was keeping her distance from her dad as well. It wasn't long before she made it clear that she was finished with her parents' weird and idiosyncratic ideas. She drew her lines in the sand, carved out her own path, and left behind their foolish imaginings and the pressure she felt to please them.

All the while, Constance was becoming increasingly aware of the desperate needs in the world around her. Taking this to heart, she determined to do what she could to improve things for others. Along with several like-minded friends, she decided to pursue community-service training, and when she was old enough, she moved out and found a position at The Social Repair Center where she lent a remarkable beauty to everything she set her hand to. Whether she welcomed clients or developed innovative ways to deliver aid to the needy, Constance carried a glinting light and graciousness wherever she went. Although sheathed in a thickening toughness, there was a beauty in Constance that nonetheless drew others to her. And, there was something inside her that longed to give away more than she knew she had.

---

2 One might suppose that other extremely bright and inquisitive young people would seek out its meaning in our world as well — if they have been *Wondering* about it, that is.

Faye and Frank looked upon their daughter's work from a distance, but with tender admiration. They were so proud of the way she would pour herself into the lives of others, but her parents were also deeply saddened, for Constance would not open up the well of her soul to them. Nor would she allow them to pour their love into her as they had in the past. Constance had ceased to believe in them.

So, there it was.

This was how things stood.

Faye had to live with the reality that no matter how hard they had tried to preserve the sacred space of their daughter's heart and imagination, they had failed. *She* had failed.

Faye stood by the sink that early summer afternoon, rooted to the floor as this reality permeated her soul. She felt that persistent old jab under her ribs along with its accompanying ache in the pit of her stomach and the faint hissing voice in her head. Despite the reality of what they had all shared together and how desperately Faye had fought to keep that alive, Constance had lost *Wonder*.

Faye faulted herself.

She took a deep breath and let it out slowly. What a relief it was for her to look out onto her gardens and see new life. The house upkeep that desperately needed her attention would have to wait, for the out-of-doors called to her. Here she found fresh perspective and encouragement as she walked among her flowers, pulling out the weeds and digging her fingers into the soil. The blossoms were always hinting at something that made her want to be with them. So she finished the dishes and wiped her hands, her bangle bracelets jingling as she headed out to the backyard. The day seemed pregnant.

The warmth of the afternoon sun fell upon her shoulders like a comforting blanket, as if her long-departed mother had come alongside her with an affectionate, knowing embrace. The effect was potent and instantaneous. She thought she had cried all her tears of grief and regret, but that wretched ache hit her stomach again as another sob erupted from inside her. She felt herself bend over involuntarily as if to deliver it to the earth. Right on cue, her nose let loose with the contents of her sinuses and she stuffed her hands into the floppy pockets of her hippy-styled gypsy pantaloons, groping for a hankie.

"It figures," she cried out. "No tissues! Now I'll have to go inside . . ."

She delved more deeply into her pockets, fingering the linings furiously as if she could make a tissue appear. No, there was no chance of that.

"But what's this?" she asked herself. Faye's sensitive fingertips discerned a teensy hard, almondy-shaped thing. "Hmmm, I wonder what this could be?"

For some reason she was intrigued by this little bit of something. She wiped her nose on her peasant-blouse sleeve as she took the little thing out and held it up to the light. Squinting in the sunshine, she examined her discovery at length.

It was a Seed.

How odd! Why would it be in her pocket? And what was it about *this* Seed that was commanding her attention? Why was it in *this* pocket? She hadn't worn these crazy pants or, for that matter, seen a Seed like this . . . since . . . why, of course!

Since . . . *Wonder*!

As she looked at it, she *knew* this Seed was one of those tiny brown-coated ladies with whom she had exploded out of Madame Yorav. They had all been thrown down to *Wonder*'s surface together! That must have been how this seed wound up in her pocket.

Her thoughts unrolled.

"Receive The Seed," she could hear Mr. Keeze say.

He had faded more and more from her mind over the year since Constance's fateful declaration, but now he was so real in her memory that he could have been standing right next to her.

"*Wosdim*," she laughed, recalling his array of mixed-up *Wonder* words. "He unlocked so much *wisdom*, for me. But what happened? I've made so many mistakes. It all went so wrong."

She placed the extraordinary little life-carrier carefully in the palm of her hand and gazed at it. A wave of remorse hit her and she started to tear up again. She heard a comforting voice stop her mid way through her guilt-trip.

"There *there*, my dear, do you know who you are? Why, you . . . *you* are *Mrs. Amazing*! Yes, you are . . . for you have dared your children to *Wonder*, and every child needs a mother like that. You see, to *truly Wonder* is to find *Artifex*. And to find *Artifex* is to be *utterly found*." These had been the very words that The Gate Keeper had whispered into her ear just before he said goodbye!

This was The Seed he had planted in her.

Faye was overwhelmed once again by recollections of the waves of pure love flowing down upon her through the majestic red door that hovered in the sky above her in that *Wonderous* flower field.

"But Mr. Keeze," Faye spoke out loud, "she doesn't *Wonder* anymore. I've failed her. There's no hope."

The voice of The Gatekeeper carried on in her head.

"Mrs. Amazing, remember! There is a marvelous secret hidden in The Seed: Even when humans are not championed by selfless love, even when you fail each other, *The Intention* of *Artifex* is still buried in the soil of every life. When *The Seed* penetrates even the most forsaken of hearts, at first it seems to die but . . . it awakens. So, in *The Seed*, there is *always* Hope."

She received his words and allowed them to penetrate. *Deep*, they were going deep, and this time she would *not* let them go. She swallowed them up, ingesting their very essence with fierce determination. She thought she could hear a familiar hissing voice scream bitterly and trail off into the distance as if it were running away, terrified and angry. The persistent ache below her solar plexus was disappearing.

She looked down at the germ of life she held in her hand and suddenly felt anticipation rise in her as if it might burst open at any second and sprout right there. She began to contemplate the possibilities.

"Where one seed has been smothered and choked-out, perhaps there is room for another . . . "

At this, an inspiration hit her. She tightly clasped her hand closed and ran into the house. Riffling through her unkempt kitchen drawers she grabbed a lock-zip snack bag. Opening her hand, she took out The Seed and dropped it into the plastic bag, sliding her fingers across the top to close it securely. Then she stuffed the bag into her pants pocket, grabbed her backpack, and keys, and headed out to the car.

About an hour later she pulled up in front of Constance's little apartment complex. It was a weathered building with a covered front porch and a patch of lawn. Although it was more than a bit run-down, it possessed an artsy charm that Constance and her room-mates thought was cool. Her daughter had done her best to spruce it up outside, putting in some plants in the tiny flower beds bordering the porch. Although they were not particularly robust, Constance's plantings had held their own.

It was late in the afternoon now and her eldest was still at work. Faye got out of her car, stood in front of the building for a moment, and then walked up the cracked sidewalk until she reached the dirt that bordered the porch.

Kneeling down, she threw her fingers into the soil between Constance's plants and began to break up the dry ground. It eventually yielded to Faye's strong fingers. She was encouraged to discover that underneath the hardened and fatigued top layer of earth, there was a more promising layer of somewhat richer, moister soil. Once she uncovered it, she took the plastic bag out of her pocket, unzipped it, and gingerly emptied its contents into her palm. Pinching the teensy seed in her fingers, she pressed it into the small hole she had just created. Then she tucked it away under a layer of dirt and patted the top lovingly as if she were putting a child to bed.

She spoke tenderly to The Seed:

"Here you are, little life, a place to grow. Please . . . awaken . . . soon."

She arose, brushed off her hands, and walked to the side of the building where she found the water spigot and, attached to it, just enough hose to reach the bed. She turned on the water and dragged the hose around the corner. With her thumb partially capping off the top of the opening, she created a water shower and directed it over

The Seed's burial place. Once the ground was sufficiently wet, she returned the hose, turned off the water, and headed to the car. There was a spring in her step.

"*Artifex be extolled!*" she sang out in her crackling voice.

She was calm and hopeful, somehow . . . free.

In the end, Mrs. Amazing had planted a seed of *Wonder* in her daughter's life, and that was enough.

EPILOGUE

IT HAD BEEN A LONG DAY AT THE SOCIAL REPAIR CENTER. Constance, who was employed there, was working with families in crisis and developing programs for children who had no one to advocate for them. She thought about her job as she navigated through the traffic. She loved summertime because it would still be light when she arrived home that evening.

Constance worked hard each day to make a difference. Progress with her clients was painstakingly slow, but at least she was doing something. She didn't agree with the uniformity demanded of the participants in the relief programs, but there had to be compromises in order to serve the greater good of The State. The Leaders knew best and had a prescribed plan. Yes, she and her family had enjoyed great freedom to think outside the box, but then, look where that had led them? Further into their delusions. She preferred to live in the real world knowing that one could not count on unicorns and rainbows in order to solve real problems. Not everyone had the luxury of indulging in fantasies. The playing field had to be leveled for all the kids who didn't have both parents and a safe place to grow. She wouldn't sit back in a bubble and leave people in crisis without assistance.

Constance was exhausted and drained as she headed up her walkway. Stopping at the mailbox that hung on the front porch post of her little apartment building, she opened the squeaky-hinged lid of the metal box and reached inside. Glancing down upon her recent attempt at gardening, her eyes fell upon a very strange flower that had sprung up among her plantings. This bloom was unlike any other in her array, and yet it seemed familiar. It was so captivating that she could hardly take her eyes off it. Its unusual qualities and dynamic colors were a delight to her weary eyes.

What was it about this flower? She had to get closer. When she walked over and bent down to look at it, a delicious floral bouquet reached out to her, unleashing in her a craving for more. She watched as a bumble bee landed on the bloom and sunk into it. Constance detected buzzy, slurping sounds as it drank, and she could *feel* the utter pleasure of the bee! How was this possible?

But it *was* possible — she was actually feeling the enjoyment of the creature! She watched, enchanted, as it contentedly flew away listing to the left and right as if drunk on honey wine. Suddenly, Constance bent over and thrust her face into the heart of the exotic blossom. She herself was longing to drink something in. Now she was engulfed in the softness of its petals, vibrating color, and overwhelming fragrance, so much so that it almost bowled her over.

Constance closed her eyes and breathed deeply, again and again. She was drenched in the sensation of being covered in an orangey-yellow substance that "chattered" at her and then felt as if she were flying. She soared upward and suddenly plummeted as her stomach flip-flopped. A moment later she drew in the musty scent of moist vegetation as she passed through a spongy fibrous barrier to enter the glow of a sacred chamber. There she heard fragments of ethereal, courtly music and caught flashes of glowing orbs that danced and merged, exploding with newness. Voices and memories echoed from somewhere inside her.

"Bride. You are Bride . . . *Generation* awaits you."

A floating purple orb encircled her, pressing into her heart. Pursuing. Romancing. Awakening.

A tear dribbled down her cheek.

She didn't know how long she had stood there drowning in that strange, ravishing flower, but at last, she pulled herself away, stood up, and stepped back from its potent effects.

She *had* to pull herself together.

Wiping her cheek and turning away, she walked up the steps and into the front door. What had just happened to her?

Constance wondered.

The End

for now . . .

⤙⤙⤙ Wondossary ⤚⤚⤚
or
"KEEZE TO WONDER,"
A
GLOSSARY
OF
WACKY WONDER WORDS

Ardor: Passionate love.

Artifex: An Amazing Word to research and explore.
                      Search this One out for yourself.

                      (*see* Xartief.)

Bublem Eeb: Why, a Bumble Bee, of course!

Cluine: Nuclei in the plant ovule. These are female
                      reproductive cells. When these cells merge with
                      the sperm cells in Generation, they produce
                      a fertilized egg or plant embryo and its first
                      nourishment. In *Wonder* The Bride Cluine
                      Orb is the egg cell and the Sisters are the other
                      female reproductive cells.

                      (*see* Uveol.)

Dartet: Tetrad. The mature pollen grain. A male
                      part of the plant. In *Wonder*, the pollen tet-
                      rads vocalize about their nifty "sporopolle-
                      nin" coating as they mature and erupt out of
                      the Microsporangia.

(*see* Llopen, *see* Microspangoria,
see Tapetum.)

Down and Dig: A fun way to describe the activity of the pollen
tubes as they penetrate the stigma and travel
down the inside of the style, up into the ovary,
and into the ovule to deposit the sperm cells
for fertilization/generation.

(*see* Mistag, *see* Lyste, *see* Yorav,
see Uveol.)

Enmast: Stamen. The stamen is a male part of the
flower. It is a stalk that grows out of the center
of the flower and is topped off by an anther.
Stamen, filament and anther form the male
part of the flower.

(see Raneth.)

Flower: A blossom or a bloom. Flowers are beautiful!
They bring us so much pleasure. Flowers are
also the reproductive structures of plants. They
produce seeds, which are new little plants.

Generation: Generation: The fertilization of the egg cells
in the female part of the plant by the sperm
cells from the male part of the plant to create a
flower zygote or embryo, which is a new little
flower alive in each seed!

He and She: He and She: The male and female parts of
flower, which are both necessary for reproduction which is generating or creating new
life! New life only occurs with the glorious
merging of male and female into one another.
Imagine the beauty of how this and how YOU
were created!

Intention: The thing that is planned. An aim, purpose,
                      or design.

Llopen: Pollen. Pollen is a male part of the plant. It's a
                      sticky, powdery substance made up of pollen
                      grains. Pollen grains produce the plant sperm
                      cells that merge with the plant egg cells to gen-
                      erate plant embryos, new baby plants!

                      (*see* Down and Dig.)

Llopen Tube-slide: Pollen Tubes. These tubes are a male part of
                      the plant. They grow out of the pollen grains
                      and penetrate the stigma of the flower, travel
                      down the inside of its style and into the ovary
                      and up and inside of the ovule to deposit the
                      sperm cells into the egg cells for fertilization/
                      generation.

                      (see Stigma, see Style, see Knight/Squire/
                      Lantern, see Generation.)

Llopinator: Pollinator. Pollinators such as birds or insects
                      (like Miss Bublem Eeb!) transfer pollen grains
                      from the male part of a plant to the female
                      part so that fertilization/Generation can
                      take place.

                      (*see* Generation.)

Lyste: Style. The style is a female part of the flower.
                      It is generally a tubelike structure. It sticks up
                      in the center of the flower and it is topped off
                      by the stigma. The style connects the stigma
                      to the ovaries of the flower where the ovules
                      or flower eggs are. Pollen Tubes pass down
                      and into the ovaries of the flower through the
                      middle of the style to fertilize the ovules/eggs

in what is called generation and this results in a new baby flower hidden in each seed!

All of the female parts of the flower together (the style, stigma and ovary) may be referred to as the pistil. Carpels are individual ovary structures within the flower and there are several of these within each pistil.

(see Mistag, see Llopen Tube-Slide, see Yorav.)

Megaspangorium: Mega*sporangium.* This is a female part of the plant that is located inside the Ovary. The Megasporangium sac is the ovule where the mature egg and sperm cells merge to generate a new flower embyro. The ovule is a chamber inside of which the nuclei divide and produce the mature egg cells of the flower. In *Wonder,* the Cluine dance, divide, and merge.

(*see* Yorav, *see* Cluine, *see* Uveol.)

Microspangoria: Micro*sporangia.* These are male parts of the plant that are located inside of the anthers. Microsporangia are tubelike structures that produce spores out of which pollen develops. This process involves the activity of tape-tum, diploid cells, sporophytes, and a kind of cell division called meiosis. In *Wonder* the "Microspangoria" sing about this as they produce pollen.

Meiosis: A type of cell division during the production of pollen grains. The "Microspangoria" in *Wonder* sang about this inside Sir "Raneth."

(*see* Micospangoria, *see* Raneth.)

Mistag: Stigma. The stigma is a female part of the flower that sits on top of the style. The sticky stigma receives pollen — it was the limey landing pad in the story! Then pollen tubes enter the stigma and travel down through the style and into the ovaries of the flower where generation takes place in the ovule.

(see Lyste, see Llopen Tube Slide, see Yorav, see Generation, see Uveol.)

Orbs: A fanciful way to describe the egg and sperm cells, which generate the new plant embryo. In *Wonder*, these cells/orbs are also called by other names such as Knight, Squire, Lantern, Bride, and Sisters to help describe their unique functions in a fun and simple way.

Raneth: Anther. The anther is a male part of the flower and is the top of the stamen. Pollen is produced on the anther in the Microsporangia.

(*see* Llopen, *see* Microspangoria.)

Scent: "The scent . . . has been sent." The scent is the fragrance emitted by the flower to draw pollinators to itself. This aroma advertises that yummy nectar and pollen are available.

(*see* Tenarc, *see* Llopen, *see* Llopinator.)

Sporophyte: The diploid spore-producing phase in the life cycle of a plant that exhibits (**Diploid**) alternation of generations. (That's just a fancy way of describing the important stuff that happens when pollen is being produced in the anther of a flowering plant. The "Microspangoria" in *Wonder* sing about this inside "Sir Raneth."

(*see* Micospangoria, *see* Raneth.)

Sporopollenin: A big fat word for the outer wall of the pollen grain.

(*see* Llopens.)

Tapetum: A specialized layer of nutritive cells found within the Megasporangium, particularly within the anther of flowering plants. The "Microspangoria" in *Wonder* sang about this inside Sir "Raneth."

(*see* Micospangoria, *see* Raneth.)

Tenarc: Nectar. Nectar is a sugary liquid produced by plants, which attracts and nourishes pollinators.

(*see* Llopinator.)

Uveol: Ovule. Ovule means "small egg." Ovules are found in the female part of the plant. An ovule is a sac in which the female reproductive cells develop and are fertilized by the male sperms cells to generate new life. Fertilized eggs are called zygotes or embryos. They are new little living plant lives! They become seeds!

(*see* Cluine, *see* Orbs, *see* Generation.)

Xartief: (*see* Artifex.)

Yorav: Ovary. A female part of the plant that contains
the ovule.

(*see* Uveol.)

The author recommends:
A video of the Reproductive Cycle of the Flowering Plant:

"The Amazing Lives of Plants"
by Dr. Larry Jensen

Published by McGraw-Hill, a business unit of The McGraw-Hill Companies, Inc.
1221 Avenue of the Americas, New York, NY 10020.

Here's a really cool flower dissection video for older kids so you can see all the parts: https://www.youtube.com/watch?v=493WeySyf-8

Here's a fun flower reproduction video for younger kids: https://www.youtube.com/watch?v=djPVgip_bdU

And here's one about seed germination as well: https://www.youtube.com/watch?v=TE6xptjgNR0